# BLASPHEMY

## DIANE NARRAWAY

# WARNING

This book is blasphemous and contains references to drug use, alcoholism, animal cruelty, racism, homophobia, amputation, rape, child abuse, infanticide, paedophilia, cults, abortion, violence, and sexual abuse including sodomy.

Most importantly, this book is fictional.

Edited by Toni Glitz
glitzedit.co.uk

Cover image by Kayla Mavrakis

Veneficia Publications

978-1-916756-12-0

March 2024

VENEFICIA PUBLICATIONS UK

veneficiapublications.com

# CONTENTS



## PROSECUTION

# DEFENCE

Angels, demons, djinn and humans
are all created by the same gods;
therefore, we have no reason to believe any god is compassionate.

# CHAPTER I
## AN INVITATION

With a final flourish of the host's quill, the ornately handwritten invitations were complete.

*You have been carefully and especially selected to dine at*
*Lucretia's on the Hill*
*Easton Boulevard*
*Los Angeles*

*13th April 2024 at 7pm sharp*
*Formal attire is optional, attendance is not!*

Everything had to be perfect, ooze wealth, and reek of decadence. These invitations were rare, and the reader had to know it. After all, they were not being cordially invited, they were being summoned.

*Attendance is not optional.* This was a warning, as failure to attend the event had consequences. There had been a few occasions in the past when someone had failed to attend. For the host, this had proved both an annoyance and an inconvenience—for the absentee, the repercussions were far greater.

There was no denying that selection was an easier process on occasions when a member declined the host's offer, but it was not meant to be easy. *Twelve good men and true,* wasn't that how the saying went?

This year, the accompanying letter also had to be worded very carefully, so as to leave no room for error. This year, God willing, there would be twelve.

*To Our Most Esteemed Guest,*

*A rare opportunity has arisen for one unique individual. After great consideration, I feel that you have the potential to be the candidate we are looking for.*

*There are twelve of you invited to this event, and should you be selected as 'the one', I guarantee this will change your and your family's lives forever.*

*We can assure you, that neither you, nor your family will ever want for anything again.*

*I look forward to meeting all of you.*

*Yours faithfully,*

*Your Host*

Each letter was placed in a silver envelope, stamped on the back with an impressive looking seal, and sent out the same day to be hand-delivered by courier, along with the necessary travel arrangements and documents.

The invitations were dispatched across the globe; the destination was nowhere near as important as the recipients—a seemingly random selection of individuals, apparently unconnected to either their host or each other.

The host flicked through the blue folder on the table. It was always prudent to know something about one's guests. Especially in situations like this.

They perused the list of recipients, committing key details to memory.

The host smiled approvingly.

"It's beautiful, exquisite even, but then I would expect nothing less, my friend. Tell me, Sam, have you read the dossier on this year's guests?"

"I have. Quite remarkable, isn't it? The similarities are uncanny."

The host nodded silently, aware that the guests were now arriving.

He could easily spot who was who. Danyl stood out like a sore thumb, but then homeless junkies are easy to spot anywhere—one looking much like another. Despite Danyl's best efforts, the nice suit he'd borrowed did little for the wearer when accompanied by the tell-tale, grey pallor from years of heroin addiction.

Ruby was just as obvious, oozing glamour and confidence, as were Simon and Ben, but then these people were used to exclusive invitations and high-class venues.

However, one should never judge a book by the cover.

"Welcome, welcome. Please take a seat. You will find your place name, but you can swap, they are merely there to prevent you from taking my seat." Both the host and Sam laughed.

Those who had arrived smiled politely as they took their places. Two younger, very striking looking men entered the room. They had met outside and were obviously quite relaxed with each other. Although their clothing was more Marketplace than Fifth Avenue, they were nonetheless quite beautiful.

"Ekansh and Julian, I presume?"

They were immediately followed by an attractive but bookish looking woman who, although she had bought an expensive dress, did not wear it well, and as a result appeared somewhat trashy. The Vatican had many things, but a sense of fashion wasn't one of them.

"I guess you really can't make a silk purse out of a sow's ear," Sam muttered, just loud enough for the host to hear.

"Indeed, it would seem not," the host replied quietly, smiling as the woman approached him. "Glad you could make it Isobella, and may I say what a lovely outfit that is."

The woman's whole face lit up as she beamed back at him. Sam, on the other hand, bit his lip and winked at her as she passed him. Better that, he figured, than to insult her by laughing.

"Take a moment," the host instructed his friend, before adding, "and be grateful she isn't wearing a wimple."

While Sam composed himself, three other guests arrived; a large, thick set man, smartly dressed in a fairly cheap tuxedo—what one might call casually classy. He did not carry himself well; slightly hunched, his eyes darted around the room as though he was constantly on the lookout. The host instantly recognised and greeted this man as Lewis.

The other two men seemed far more relaxed and casually chatted to each other, before the host interrupted them.

"Good evening ... Gerry?" the host inquired, and Gerry nodded in return. "Ah, a man of few words I see."

Gerry looked cross. He understood that he was being laughed at, and did not like it. "Please be seated," the host gestured amiably towards the table.

A large, good-looking man extended his hand out to the host, who smiled in return and enthusiastically accepted it. The man came across as a gentle giant, slightly dishevelled but at least clean and tidy.

"Welcome, Nathan. Please find your seat, the places are all named."

Eventually the last two guests appeared.

"Ah, welcome, welcome. Andros?" He shook the hand of an exquisitely dressed older man. Everything about Andros screamed wealth. This man was not born with a silver spoon in his mouth, he was self-made and he wore that success on his sleeve, like lovers wear their hearts.

"And last but by no means least, Zack." Zack half smiled and begrudgingly shook the host's hand. Zack was the polar opposite of Andros, Simon, Ruby and Ben. His poverty was as important to him as their success was to them. His clothes were faded and grubby, and he looked as though he would be more at home with Danyl on the streets, but for his healthy complexion.

"All of them this time," the host whispered to Sam, nudging him gently. "This year will be quite a treat, I think. Don't you?"

Sam nodded, his eyes twinkling with delight.

As the guests settled into their seats, their host positioned himself at the head of the table. He was as well dressed as his more refined guests, with an ethereal allure; quite captivating to look at.

The guests waited in silence for him to speak, but instead of any formal greeting, the sound of heavy locks clanking into place reverberated around the room, and was immediately echoed by a series of gasps from the guests as, ashen-faced, they looked first around the room and then at each other. Some were paralysed with fear, others rose as if to demand release, but no words came out—fight, flight or freeze, all were futile.

"Sit down!" bellowed their host at those who had dared to stand.

It was hard to decide which instilled more fear; their host or the dreadful silence that now hung heavily in the air, thick with panic and confusion.

The host immediately returned to his composed, calm demeanour, as his eyes flashed from one guest to another. Slowly, they returned to their seats—none daring to break the silence—their voices crippled with panic. They looked for exits but saw none.

"I think it's time I introduce your hosts for the evening and explain why you have all been invited here tonight."

The host took a sip of water, before continuing.

"I am known by many names. Some call me the Angel of Death, others the Grim Reaper. I prefer Azrael. Our maître d' tonight is my oldest friend, Samael." Azrael waved his hand towards a well-dressed, tall, dark, and handsome man. The type of man fortune tellers talk about and women dream of. "You will be waited on by the three younger daughters of Iblis—his two elder daughters are guarding the kitchen. You do not want to mess with the djinn, especially not shayāṭīn."

Azrael gestured towards the kitchen and twelve pairs of eyes followed his indication, settling on three identical young women. The three younger daughters—triplets, every man's fantasy. Some of the guests relaxed, until they spotted the older two, who were definitely not so appealing. They appeared far more formidable and were clearly a force to be reckoned with.

"Yes, you are all locked in," Azrael continued, pulling their attention back. "The only open door is to the kitchen, and in the unlikely event you should get that far, you will find it leads nowhere.

Now, let me explain why you are here."

The room was silent, the air still thick with fear. The guests' heartbeats could be heard above the clanking of pans and dishes coming from the kitchen. Azrael had command of the room.

"None of you will know this. You couldn't, it was so long ago. You are here because you are direct descendants of the twelve tribes of Israel. I can tell by the looks on your faces that this means nothing to most of you. Hell! Most of you are atheists."

Simon rose from his seat and opened his mouth to comment but Azrael glared at him.

"Sit down, you sanctimonious fool. I am fully aware of your *Christian piety*, and I know, far better than you, just how much your god forgives, and how fiercely he loves his flock.

About 4,000 years ago, a pious man named Jacob lived with his two wives, Leah and Rebeka, along with his wives' handmaidens. He fathered a total of twelve sons and one daughter. His twelve sons were the founders of the twelve tribes of Israel. Unlike Jacob, his sons were not so devout, and each one transgressed in some way or another. Most are mentioned in the Old Testament, but not all. What was never mentioned was Yahweh's wrath and the judgement he passed on all twelve tribes.

Yahweh was a minor desert god with a God complex. Jacob was one of Yahweh's chosen people, and as such, Yahweh expected more from Jacob's sons. Such was his anger, that he demanded a sacrifice from them—a human sacrifice. One man or woman from one tribe would be sacrificed every one hundred years.

Of course, Jacob pleaded with Yahweh on behalf of his sons. Yahweh loved Jacob and therefore promised that no innocent blood would ever be shed. Instead, he decided that those chosen to be sacrificed would be those most deserving of such a fate.

This year one of you will be that sacrifice, and you are also, albeit ironically, the twelve good men who will decide which one of you it will be."

A deathly stillness blanketed the room as the colour drained from the guests' faces.

Azrael, Samael, and the shayāṭīn flashed glances at each other and around the room at each of the guests, and watched their reactions as the reality of their situation became apparent.

In those first few minutes when it dawns on a person that this may well be the end of their life—that they may only have a few hours left to live— they are either blessed with moments of true clarity, or their thoughts become confused and chaotic. There is rarely anything in between, as their lives are laid out before them. Guilt and shame are commonplace, but fear more so.

Those among the guests who had the ability to think clearly began to consider their options. There were no exits, so finding an alternative way to save themselves was paramount— life was so much more precious when it was being snatched away. Those whose thoughts were more chaotic remained frozen and stunned, unable to properly digest what was happening but equally aware they were about to lose something they cherished more than anything else.

There is only one treasure greater than one's life, the closer death comes, and that is one's soul.

That dreadful silence lingered for a moment or two, before being broken by their host, judge and possibly their executioner.

"I believe the hors d'oeuvres are ready," Azrael announced. "As always, they are a dish best served cold, with a cocktail, in this instance *Death by Sex.*"

# PROSECUTION

# CHAPTER II
## RUBY



*Owner of Rubies, one of Beverly Hills' hottest night spots.
A nightclub with pole dancers, private dancers, and above all, A-list clientele.
Wealthy, promiscuous and single.*

"Let us begin with you, Ruby, from the Tribe of Reuben. You are descended from Reuben, a man who slept with his mother's handmaid, or if you prefer, his stepmother. Such an action was bound to have consequences. He slept with another man's woman and the bible teaches that this is an abomination. Jacob cursed Reuben on his deathbed, that he would no longer excel, but the biblical version, as always, is only partially true. Reuben was exiled and the land he and his tribe were given was barren. Many of his tribe died of starvation and he did not see old age. His descendants, too, were cursed to suffer hardship and hunger—success would not come easily.

You own a prestigious nightclub with all the extras imaginable, catering to the rich and famous. Your discretion is legendary. Less well known is your own love life. One shouldn't mix business with pleasure, should one?

You have had many lovers: some male, some female and some, well let's just say alternative. Some are free and some you pay for. Anything goes as long as there is no commitment. And love, well that doesn't come into it at all. Not these days. Who was the last person you cared about?

You grew up in a violent household. Your father left when you were four years old, tired of being abused by your mother. It was only a couple of months later that her drunken temper found its way to you. That is something no child should ever have to go through."

Ruby's eyes filled with tears. This was her shame. How dare this stranger share her past with others.

"Oh, you might be well respected now, but as a little girl you were less than nothing in the eyes of your mother. It was only your kind, elderly neighbour, Mrs Bernstein, who took pity on you. Do you remember? You called her Mamaw.”

Ruby nodded. Of course, she remembered Mamaw. She was from St Louis, and always treated her kindly. These were such painful memories.

“It was Mamaw who found you bloodied and bruised the first time your mother beat you. Do you remember how she carried you to the welfare clinic and got you the help you needed? That’s where you met Dr Angela. Nobody cared about little girls from Skid Row, but Mamaw and Dr Angela did. Didn’t they?”

Tears streamed down Ruby’s face. She had repressed her childhood memories—more importantly, she had left Skid Row behind and traded it for Beverly Hills. She had buried all that pain and hurt under a mountain of expensive cocktails and even more expensive lovers. Her world was disposable: disposable income, disposable staff and most importantly, disposable lovers, and she liked it that way. The past should remain buried.

Azrael, unmoved by her tears and obvious anguish, continued.

“By the time you were six Mamaw had died, and you were taking yourself regularly to Dr Angela's clinic. She was your only friend. You called her Dr Guardian Angel, do you remember? She always patched you up and fed you before letting you leave her clinic. And when you were old enough, she and her husband, Grant, helped you leave Skid Row.

Do you remember Dr Angela's death? The tragedy, and indeed, the irony."

"Stop! I don't care who you are, that's enough. Dredge up my childhood if you must but this is my cross to bear, no one else's."

"But you don't bear it, do you Ruby? Exhibit A please Sam."

Samael handed a couple of photos to each of the guests. One was of a small girl with fresh bruises covering her face and body, and a scar on her lower back from where her mother had pushed her and she had caught herself on some broken glass. The other was a crime scene photograph of a woman hanging. Stapled to it was an accompanying letter. The letter stated that the woman had taken her own life as she was unable to bear her husband's infidelity. Signed by Dr Angela Benedict.

"I wasn't the first," Ruby mumbled.

"No Ruby, you weren't, but you were the last. She loved you. She was always kind to you. She was there when nobody else cared about you and you repaid her, how? By fucking the man she loved. He may not have been worthy of her, but you should have been. You truly are a descendant of Reuben, aren't you?

Tell me Ruby, is that how you measure success? By destroying the life of your Guardian Angel. By causing her death. Do you know how long it took for her to die? How long she hung there, gasping for breath. Choking. Wishing death would come quicker, with the light slowly draining out of her. Tell me why you should live, while someone who helped so many little children like you, deserved to die.

That day, four people died who might otherwise have lived. One little girl wasn't much older than you were when Mamaw took you there all those years ago. Exhibit B please."

Samael handed each guest a photograph of a dead five-year-old lying in an alley.

"She died of sepsis and hypothermia. L.A. may not be the coldest place on Earth, but it can get cold at night. This poor child was beaten, half-starved, and cold."

The photograph was accompanied by the sound of the child's sobs as they grew fainter, and fainter, before eventually stopping. The silence was even more chilling than the image.

All eyes were on Ruby and she knew there was nothing she could say, because there were no excuses.

# CHAPTER III
## SIMON

*Dallas gynaecologist, regular church goer.*
*Highly respected by his peers. Very outspoken*
*in his views on abortion.*
*Married with a daughter.*

"I see many of you have not touched your food. Perhaps this course will be more to your liking. It is the amuse bouche:  Devilled Eggs served with Eau de Vie.

Simon, you are a descendant from the tribe of Simeon. Your ancestral crimes include genocide and treachery. Convincing himself that he was avenging his sister's rape, Simeon dishonoured his father's treaty and tricked an entire tribe into circumcision. While they were still weak with pain, he, along with his brother Levi, slaughtered all the menfolk. His other brothers took anything of value, including the women and children.

Let us now examine your crimes, although I am quite certain

you do not believe you are guilty of anything."

Simon stared coldly at Azrael.

"This is ridiculous, I am a man of science, I worship God and pay my taxes. You have nothing on me. I am not like some long-forgotten ancestor, or Ruby."

"And I am sure you believe that, but let us look a little closer. You grew up with all the privileges afforded to young, white, Christian males in the US. A good education, Harvard, no less. A pretty—although more importantly, virginal—wife, and a daughter. Not to mention that beautiful house, luxury car, and that six-figure obstetric gynaecologist's income. However, most important is your standing in the community and your place in heaven, which must surely be secured for you by now.

And my, didn't you just last fall, buy a painting in a charity auction for several thousand dollars? Your contribution will no doubt help all those poor orphans."

"It was a charitable act—what is wrong with that? You can't condemn me for trying to help God's children."

Azrael's laughter echoed around the room.

"Oh, I'm sure you believe that, I really am," he mocked, trying to stifle his laughter. "You swore an oath when you graduated did you not?" Azrael regained his composure.

Simon nodded, having opted not to add any further comments for the time being. He did not appreciate being ridiculed; certainly not in front of others, who he considered mostly to be beneath him.

"Tell me, did that oath not include something along the lines of *Where possible I vow to save life and promote the health and comfort of my patient,* and doesn't it include the line, *for all those who entrust themselves into my care*? Blah blah blah. I expect you meant that once too, didn't you?

So, what happened when SCOTUS voted to overturn the Wade vs Roe decision, and Texas outlawed abortion? The laws were extreme initially, but in September gynaecologists were given the right to operate on women with ectopic pregnancies, before they became life threatening. Tell me Simon, have you earned your place in heaven?

A young girl, around 16-years-old, was brought in to see you. Her father was concerned and said he would pay anything to save her. You took his money and said you would do everything you could. You did everything right and you found it was an ectopic pregnancy. All you had to do was remove the fallopian tube and she would survive, but you didn't. You kept her there for another couple of days, all at Daddy's expense, and eventually the tube ruptured, and she died. Cause of death was recorded as internal haemorrhage; it should have said malice and neglect. Like your ancestor, you deceived her father into believing you could help her, and instead you let her die.

The worst part is that she wasn't the only one you allowed to die. There are at least two children in that orphanage you donated to, whose mothers died unnecessarily. It wasn't all about money, I know, it was your own insane beliefs. In some way you believed you were doing Yahweh's bidding.

These women were ill, they had medical conditions. They needed treating, not abandoning. Exhibit A in the case of Simon, a recording of the young girl—I believe her name was Dinah—as her body is poisoned following the rupture of her fallopian tube. There is also a copy of the bank transfer made directly to her doctor. Simon." Azrael gestured toward the somewhat uncomfortable looking Texan doctor sitting across the table.

The guests sat in silence, listening to the chilling screams and sobs of the young girl, before she finally succumbed to death.

"Tell me Simon, I'm curious, were you expecting that misplaced embryo to slide down the tube and reposition itself in the womb? Of course not. Or perhaps you believe that their deaths must be the will of your god, otherwise he would have saved them, wouldn't he? Or maybe, just maybe, you could have saved them, like any other compassionate human being. What do you think Samael? Which god do you think he was working for?"

Samael smiled. "That's easy—none."

# CHAPTER IV
## LEWIS

*A soldier from London, in active service during the Gulf War. Discharged due to injury, now employed as an odd-job man at a nursing home.*
*Husband to a deceased wife, and Father to two deceased sons.*

The waitresses cleared away the plates, most of which were untouched, although all the glasses were empty.

"What's wrong, lost your appetites? Such a shame as the food really is quite exquisite. One might even say it was heavenly. Perhaps the soup will be more to your taste. I believe it is Grandma's Gunpowder Chicken Chowder with a Side Shooter."

Lewis shifted in his seat uncomfortably, and Azrael smiled. There was little doubt that he was savouring their fear as much as he was the food.

"So, Lewis, let's take a look at why you are here. You are a descendant from the Tribe of Levi, and Levi was Simeon's accomplice in the massacre of the Canaanites. For those who do know the Bible, let me clarify one thing; those who wrote it weren't there, but I was, and my memory is unfaltering. Levi and Simeon's judgement was, shall we say, misplaced, and their actions calculated and vicious. Their sister wasn't raped, she was seduced by her alleged rapist, something her brothers could not accept.

But I digress. Let me return to you, Lewis. What did you do?"

"Served my country and got poorly repaid for it."

"Really, that's how you see it? Well, for the benefit of the jury …" Azrael smiled and his eyes became dark, menacing pools, reflecting the countless crimes of humanity. "… Lewis had an unremarkable childhood, fairly typical of those growing up in the East End of London, in a tower block during the 60's. Life wasn't easy amid the crime-riddled streets, but it wasn't especially difficult either. Your parents worked and there was always food on the table. That in itself was more fortunate than many.

To your credit, and one must give credit where it's due, you managed to avoid entering that life of crime. You were a loner and spent most of your childhood throwing stones at cans or rats, whichever was available. Rats were of course preferable, and once dead were formed into grotesque creatures resembling amputees and murder victims.

Sadly, killing rats in such a way led to a morbid fascination with death, and with it a greater understanding of life, mostly how fragile it is. By age 16, you had considered taking an apprenticeship with a local undertaker but instead you joined the army. The year was 1978.

You were married in 1986, to the first woman who came along, and following the birth of your second son in 1990, you were assigned to the 1st Armoured Brigade and sent to Iraq as part of Operation Desert Storm."

Lewis shook his head sadly.

"I loved my wife and kids, and I miss them every day."

"I'm sure you did, but where are they now?"

Lewis did not reply.

"It was during active service that your crimes began. You were no longer throwing stones at rats; you were a desert rat shooting bullets at human targets."

"I am paying for it now."

"How so?"

Azrael followed Lewis's eyes downward.

"Oh, you mean your leg? You have got to be kidding. A prosthetic leg is hardly even a downpayment on what you have done. You have taken innocent people's lives. Not soldiers, not the enemy—small children, one of whom had only just started walking.

Anyway, it was during your watch on a quiet night that you heard a muffled noise coming from little more than a hut. Inside were two small children, huddled together and sobbing. Their parents lay dead nearby. They were hungry and frightened little children, about the same age as your own. You could have called for help, a medic, got them taken to safety, but you didn't, did you Lewis?"

Lewis said nothing.

"Instead, you shot them both, and mutilated their little bodies, fashioning them into something no longer human. I'll ask again, where are your wife and children?"

Lewis still said nothing.

"And now you work doing odd jobs in a nursing home, closer to death than ever. In some curious way, this seems to have abated your disgusting need to murder and mutilate. And so, once more Lewis, where are your wife and the children you claim to love?"

Lewis looked around at the faces of the others, all of which were looking directly at him. He shook his head but remained silent.

"You see Lewis, I know where they are. However, for the benefit of everyone else, let me present exhibits A, B and C for Lewis. Samael, if you would, please."

Samael handed each guest a photograph of the two mutilated children and accompanying audio recording of the children's deaths. Their screams didn't last long but the sound of Lewis's frenzied hacking and chopping continued long enough for anyone with a spoon in their hand to put it down. Isobella puked, which was deftly caught in a bucket by the daughters of Iblis. Exhibit C, a photo of Lewis's dead wife and children came almost as a relief.

"As you can all see, shooting wasn't quite enough; not as thrilling as stoning rats to death—but stoning your family to death—well, that seemed to do the trick. As to their location, they are in a disused cellar. I believe they are in the one beneath the nursing home you work in, are they not?"

And despite the odd gasp of horror, still Lewis said nothing.

# CHAPTER V

## JULIAN

*Flamboyant member of Berlin society; a charming socialite, popular with the ladies, not so popular with the authorities. No steady girlfriend, no children he admits to.*

"Time for the next course. An appetizer: Shanghaied Sweet Meat with a Berlin Vice Grip. Are you getting it yet?" Azrael fixed his attention on Julian.

"Julian from the Tribe of Judah. Your ancestor was guilty of many things. Mostly, like you, he was guilty of deceiving himself, but that is not enough to condemn a man, let alone sacrifice his descendants. No, Judah was guilty of far more than that. It is true that Judah rescued Joseph from death, but at what cost? Judah sold Joseph, his wife and his daughters into slavery. Worse still, they were sold to Pharaoh's court. The Bible doesn't mention Joseph's first wife. She, along with her daughters, were raped and sodomised repeatedly. Oh yes, Joseph survived, not only because he could

34

interpret dreams, but because he had a penchant for men, and Pharaoh took a shine to him. Judah knew he was condemning Joseph's wife and daughters to death and that was his crime.

You see, fellow guests ... jurors ... Julian comes from a colourful, seemingly enviable background—"

"You would see my childhood as enviable. I would have had more parental attention if I'd been Ruby."

"Interesting comparison," Azrael mused. "However, I said seemingly, as I am sure many of your peers would have seen your upbringing as enviable. Your father was a black navvy whose family had come to Berlin after the war. He firmly believed a man should work hard and play hard, but all too often he played more than he worked. Your mother was a nightclub singer, who worked most nights. In her early years she could have made it big, but she had you and your father holding her back. She didn't care much for either. This suited your father as he was able to do as he pleased, but for the young mixed-race Julian, life was undeniably difficult.

You spent most of your childhood around the Berlin club scene, so it was inevitable you would be introduced to gangsters and whores—the seedier side of Berlin's night life.

His disinterest in his son didn't stop him giving you unsolicited advice about the company you kept, and I bet you lost count of the number of times you caught him fucking a barmaid, chorus girl or hooker.

It didn't take you long to secure work, collecting drugs and brothel rents for Berlin's underground bosses. And let's face it, you liked it. You were, after all, your father's son. Far more than you realised."

Julian looked confused, if not disgusted, at the idea that he could be anything like his father.

"Oh, did you never wonder about all his womanising?" The comment hung in the air, just for a moment, before he continued.

"You worked your way up, introduced the new girls to the benefits of cocaine for taking the edge off that first night. And then you began recruiting girls yourself. You see, working girls aren't really people, they are *objets d'amusement,* are they not? They don't have feelings, thoughts or ambitions. They don't want the same things as real people, do they, Julian? How many times have you been their first customer? It is the pimp's job to break in any virgins, isn't it?

But it doesn't end there, does it? When business is booming, and new girls are required, what then? Why, human trafficking of course. Exactly how many girls have you stolen from loving families? Some just snatched by the roadside, others lured from poverty-stricken areas with the promise of decent, honest work. All, without exception, ended up drug addicts, riddled with disease and abused by desperate, drunken old men.

And just how many back street abortions have you sanctioned? And well, should one die of infection or drug overdose, you just replace them with another one.

And you. Look at you. Dressed like a peacock, surrounded by women, but like your father, all the whores in the world can't satisfy your appetite. So, you fill the void with cocaine and champagne, but what you really crave is a man. But oh, how that would destroy your reputation. Your social standing. So, you abuse the women you sleep with, pumping them full of heroin and then sodomising them. How many have died satisfying your homosexual needs?

The worst part is, you could have come out and nobody would have cared. But no, you chose to continue raping and murdering young women who wanted nothing more than a better life.

Please, Samael, exhibit A for the benefit of the jury."

Exhibit A in this instance, was a video of Julian injecting a very nervous young girl.

"Was she even legal?"

Julian nodded. "She was 17."

The video showed him administering her first ever shot of heroin. She flopped back onto the bed, her eyes rolling. Julian sat, waiting until she was barely conscious. He undressed her. She half-heartedly flailed her arms about but was too weak to fight him off, and eventually she gave up trying. At this point, he flipped her over and aggressively penetrated her. Despite how heavily sedated she was, the girl sobbed throughout the entire ordeal. At the end of the film there was a still image of the girl's funeral.

"She was just one of many... Still, onto the next course."

# CHAPTER VI
## ANDROS

*Olive farmer from Corfu. Successful
businessman.
Married with two daughters and four sons.*

"Now for the salad course, a spectacular Machiavellian Salata with a choice of mocktails. Please enjoy— you are my guests after all. Which brings me to Andros.

Firstly, of course, I will address the crime of his ancestor, Asher. Jacob blessed Asher saying that his bread shall be fat and that he shall yield royal dainties, or luxurious goods if you prefer. Likewise, Moses said of Asher, *May he be blessed above other sons; may he be esteemed by his brothers; may he bathe his feet in olive oil.*

Despite these wondrous blessings, it was Asher who reported Reuben's incestuous behaviour to his brothers. It is said that he did this with all good intention, but he knew that this information would reach Jacob's ears and he would gain favour with his father, and he hoped that Reuben would be disowned. Reuben did indeed lose his birthright, but it was given to Joseph. As a result, Asher suggested to his bothers that Joseph be killed, but Judah stepped in at the last minute. Jacob blessed all his sons on his deathbed, but Asher was the last to be blessed by his father. Despite receiving a favourable blessing, Asher was cruel and murdered Jacob shortly afterwards. Of course, this is not stated in the bible, but many things aren't. Asher killed many others who got in his way, yet nothing could ever be proved.

Such irony in the similarities wouldn't you say, Andros? As you sit here now before me with your feet bathed in olive oil and steeped in blood."

By this point, each guest was hoping that their crime was not as bad as either those preceding or following them.

"Now, I know Machiavellian Salata sounds more Italian than Greek but then Andros is only half Greek, his father was Italian. I urge you to try it, as it really is quite delicate. One might even say subtle.

Anyway, I digress. Andros, descendant of the tribe of Asher, grew up in the heart of Turin. His childhood was what one might consider average. His father managed a prestigious restaurant, and his mother was a waitress there. And that is where Andros met the woman who changed his life. A Greek woman who owned a thriving olive grove—Phoebe Angelos.

If you recall, Andros, you were helping in the restaurant that summer. I believe it was June 1986 and you were just 23. Phoebe was 55, around the same age as your own mother and just as delightful.

Phoebe took a shine to you and offered you work in her household, on a good wage too. And all credit where due, you worked extremely hard and proved invaluable. More importantly, you became her confidant and accompanied her to many business engagements.

Phoebe, the sole owner of one of the oldest olive groves in Corfu. She had three heirs to her fortune: her eldest son, Alexander, who was married with a young baby son, her middle son, Damian, and her daughter, Daphne.

Alexander was happily married and his baby son, Nicholas was the apple of Phoebe's eye. Damian was less settled and the same age as you, Andros, as was Damian's girlfriend, Calliope. The family viewed her as a gold digger and she wasted no time finding her way into your bed did she, Andros?"

"She is my wife. There is no crime, nor shame in that."

"No, there isn't, but allow me to continue, and please enjoy your food as our chef has gone to great lengths to make this meal ... well, special.

As I was saying, Phoebe's heirs, the youngest of which, Daphne, was a troubled girl. She was a 14-year-old when her father died of a brain tumour, and by adulthood it had taken its toll on her mental health. By 16 she was using opioids on a regular basis, and by the time she was 18 she had been in several institutions.

She was 19 when you began working there, and she was not in a good place with her drug use.

Just six months after you began work at Olea Myra Farm, Alexander and his family were killed in a car accident. Somebody had fitted a bomb to his car. The police believed it to be a threat or warning designed to make her sell up, but she had received no such offer, or threat. However, the last person anyone suspected was you, was it, Andros?

Eight months later Damian drowned following an argument with Calliope. He was exceptionally drunk and had accused her of having an affair. Their argument culminated in him hitting Calliope and throwing her out onto the street.

Alone and incredibly drunk, he carried a full bottle of vodka outside to the pool area. Halfway through the bottle, he tripped into the pool and hit his head, knocked unconscious, he drowned. But did he fall, or was he pushed? I would go with the latter. Of course, there were no witnesses, and the verdict was accidental death. It was, conveniently, Damian's younger sister, Daphne, who found him. This was no accident either, was it? There are no crimes of passion or moments of impulse because everything you do is well thought out. Calculated.

The end result of Daphne—the least stable member of the household—finding her brother was her needing to use. Unsurprisingly, on this occasion her stash was purer than usual, and she overdosed. With all the chaos surrounding her brother's death, Daphne's body was not discovered until the following morning, with the needle still perched between her toes, and a trail of dried vomit at the corner of her mouth. She had been dead for several hours.

Phoebe was still grieving the loss of her eldest son, and his wife and baby son eight months earlier. She was devastated by the loss of her other children, and it was you who helped her to her bed and dealt with the authorities. In fact, you were her rock. A tower of strength. You were undeniably someone she relied on, who had been her constant companion for the best part of a year.

Tell me, Andros, were you genuinely upset when you found her lifeless body the next morning, or were they just crocodile tears?"

"I didn't kill her, she had been good to me, why would I kill her, or her children?"

"Don't be fooled by any of this. There may not have been any obvious motive or physical evidence to convict this man." Azrael pointed to Andros, his expression betraying his anger. "But he is guilty. As guilty as sin. And no, he did not kill Phoebe, she took her own life. He had taken everything else from her, everything that mattered, and her heart was irreparably broken.

She left a suicide note apologising to you and thanking you for being her only friend. There was also a handwritten will leaving you everything. You were 24-years-old and the owner of a thriving olive grove, with an already substantial bank balance. You married Calliope and went on to father six children.

Your family are privileged but they are indeed the flesh and blood on your hands. Please, Samael, exhibits A, B and C."

Exhibit A was a video of Daphne sobbing her heart out as she loaded the needle for the final time before plunging it between her big toe and the one beside it. Moments later she began to choke, unable to move her head. Her death followed shortly.

Exhibits B and C were poor delusional Phoebe's suicide note and updated will.

# CHAPTER VII
## JAI

*Butler for a wealthy merchant in Delhi.*
*In the same employment since he was sixteen.*
*Single.*

"This brings us to the fish course. Sliced Bombay Duck and Shark Chutney, washed down with a glass of Knee Cracker Cider.

Of course, this also brings me to Ekansh, or should I say Jai? That is your birth name is it not?" Jai nodded. He had not been called Jai for many years and had almost forgotten that he had ever had that name. It was as though Azrael could read his mind.

"Your name, Ekansh, it's just glamour. A beautiful mask—Jai is always there, just beneath the surface.

Jai's ancestor was Jacob's favourite son, Joseph. Joseph found favour with his father by, on the surface, being good, honourable even. Underneath, Joseph was devious. He interpreted dreams, which were not visions from God but merely stories which served the purpose of becoming favourite. Joseph was devious, secretive and, like you, he gained favour with those in power. Exactly like you!

In Egypt, Joseph used his own sexual preferences to gain favour with the pharaoh, the guards, and indeed anyone, as long as he benefitted. Biblically, homosexuality was a sin. This was not the case in Egypt, where it was a way of life favoured by many.

Joseph was a whore and a cheat, and had no thought for the consequences of his actions. He denied his brothers, although according to all texts he relented later. He did not.

The story of Joseph is one of the most fabricated in the scriptures. He lay with men, and cheated and swindled his way to the top. It is true that he married and had two daughters, but his preference, like yours, was men.

But what of your story, Jai? You grew up in an orphanage in Delhi where your best friend was a boy named Ekansh. There's an irony to his name is there not, Jai? For the benefit of the others, Ekansh means whole, but we will get to that.

Jai and Ekansh were inseparable, they could easily have been mistaken for brothers. They shared everything, had similar tastes, and to some extent looked similar. But childish games, and adolescent fantasies soon made way for the harsh realities of life.

Many orphanages kept children until they reached 18, but not yours, Jai. You were either lucky enough to get work or you were on the streets at 16.

Ekansh was destined to be one of the lucky ones. Several months before they were due to leave, a woman from a wealthy merchant's home came to the orphanage. Initially she came to read stories to all of you, but while there she took a shine to Ekansh and said she would ask her boss if there was any work going.

Ekansh was delighted, and for a while you, too, pretended to share his happiness. But the closer it got to your sixteenth birthday, the more jealous you became. Envy is a sin for a reason, you know.

It had been six months since the woman had come to the orphanage and a message was sent to Ekansh stating that the merchant wanted to meet the boy, with a view to him starting work when he reached 16-years-old a month or so later.

That's when you reminded him of the story the woman had told: the Prince and the Pauper. You persuaded Ekansh to switch places, just for fun. After all, you would be back later that day. What was it you said? Oh yes, *I just need to make sure he is worthy of my brother, Ekansh.* Like a fool Ekansh agreed, believing every word you said. But that isn't what happened, is it?"

Jai hung his head and remained silent. He knew what was coming.

"The man who collected you had no reason to suspect you weren't Ekansh, nor did the merchant. Likewise, the woman who had spoken to Ekansh all those months ago couldn't be sure you weren't him. And so, from that moment on you became Ekansh.

The merchant found you charming, and you, realising your opportunity, seized it with both hands. You could see the merchant was attracted to you and so you took every advantage of the situation.

You allowed him full access to your young body. You abused the abuser, becoming his lover as well as a member of staff. But you weren't just any member of staff, you were his personal valet from day one. Of course, you never returned to the orphanage, and like the prince in the story, Ekansh was double-crossed and as a result, left to the mercy of the streets.

Not that I think you care, but it's hard for a young boy to make money on the streets, especially one with some morals. Unlike you, Ekansh was not homosexual and was reluctant to prostitute himself.

He had been on the streets for about a week and was hungrier than either you or he could've imagined, when he met a young blind girl. She, too, was a beggar and told him that boys like him don't last long on the street—he needed help and protection. She told him she knew someone who could help him. That it would hurt, and he wouldn't like it but at least he would get money for food.

She took him to a man she called Uncle, and he said he would help but at a price. He explained the conditions and Ekansh reluctantly agreed.

I feel this might be a good time to share exhibit A with our guests. If you don't mind, Samael."

Samael began the video. A somewhat dishevelled man handed the young lad, Jai knew to be Ekansh, a bottle of illegal street liquor, known locally as desi daru, or hooch. This was accompanied by a small shot of heroin.

"In case you're wondering, Jai, he had used that same needle on three people that night, one of which he charged for the pleasure. It was the only needle he used that week. He just kept refilling it until he could acquire a different one. And no, he didn't use it on himself."

The video continued as Ekansh passed out and the man produced a hacksaw. The blind girl held the boy's hand as Uncle began to saw his left leg, just below the knee.

All the guests winced as the saw ripped through the flesh, splintering the bone. It was old and far from fit for purpose, and Ekansh screamed in agony.

"Quiet him down," the man growled at the blind girl, and she grabbed a nearby piece of wood and held it between Ekansh's teeth. He sobbed, and despite the girl's best attempts to soothe him, his screams echoed throughout the homeless camp as Uncle sealed the wound with a burning piece of wood.

"So you see, Jai, the result of your duplicity. But it doesn't stop there does it, because you knew all that didn't you, Jai? You knew what had happened to Ekansh. The same as you also knew he died a few weeks later from septicaemia as a result. He was just 16 when he died. As for the merchant's wife ... exhibit B please, Sam."

Samael handed each of them a photo of a woman lying in a bath with blood pouring from her wrists.

"She died as a result of your affair with her husband. She saw you both in her bed—watched the whole thing from beginning to end. She saw exactly how you satisfied her husband in ways that she never could.

But tell me, Jai, did you know about the unborn child in her belly, whose life was also taken that day?"

Azrael clapped his hands and the younger daughters of Iblis hurriedly cleared away the dishes and returned to the kitchen to fetch the next course.

# CHAPTER VIII
## BEN

*Psychic medium and fortune teller in London.
Wrote several books on the subject of
spiritism, has an A-list following.
No long-term partner, no children.*

"As our first main course we have Pulled Long Pork, with After-Death sauce, served on a bed of cabbage. Just kidding its goat, wouldn't dream of serving anything not kosher! This is accompanied by a tall glass of Romany Sangria made with our very own house Rioja. Please indulge yourselves—I know I will.

So, on to Ben, descended from the Tribe of Benjamin.

The blessing of your ancestor from his father, Jacob, is written in the scriptures as *Benjamin is a ravenous wolf; In the morning he consumes the foe, and in the evening, he divides the spoil.* This blessing became the crime of your ancestor; devouring the flesh of others."

Everyone looked at Ben, who looked horrified at the implication.

"I have never—"

"I know Ben, and please, everyone, these are not Ben's crimes. Ben is absolutely not a cannibal, but his crimes, like all of yours, are no more palatable.

Ben, like his ancestor, has a rare gift—the gift of foresight. He can see the future. Tell me, how uncomfortable do you feel right now, Ben? Do you know what's coming? Of course, you don't. You have no power in here.

The young Ben was a sensitive child, much like his ancestor, and similarly was popular with the family. Ben and his ancestor have much in common, just not the cannibal thing. Ben here, is a true Romany Gypsy. He is no charlatan—his ability to predict the future is absolutely genuine, and was nurtured by his family. His gift, as they call it, has been in his family for generations. Ben's future was his destiny, written in the stars, so to speak.

However, being the *real deal* doesn't mean he hasn't exploited it for his own gain. With such a gift comes the heavy burden of responsibility and accountability. But not for you, Ben.

These rules don't apply to you, do they?"

Azrael's eyes were dark and cold as they bored deep into Ben's soul. Ben had sat at the table long enough to be terrified of what was coming. Azrael took a deep breath, redirected his gaze less menacingly at the rest of the table, and continued.

"You see, friends, Ben is a reader, a medium and a spiritist. This place, this restaurant, is less of a surprise to him than it is the rest of you. He has written books on the subject, although I doubt any here have read them: *The Dark Realms of the Spirit, The Hidden Curse of Foresight, Spiritual Shadows of the Future*. No? Didn't think so.

Ben does alright though, don't you, Ben?"

Ben looked across at Azrael, avoiding eye contact and saying nothing.

"Ben, like Ruby, has an A-list clientele. He could have been set for life, and never sat at this table, but you see, Ben is a ravenous wolf. He is a predator with an insatiable appetite for sex. He has a deep uncontrollable hunger that can never be satisfied.

Here's how it works. Nobody ... but nobody, and there are no exceptions, goes to a fortune teller when life is going well. So, as you can see, his clients are vulnerable to begin with, and while manipulating a few celebrities into sleeping with you isn't ethical, it's hardly enough to get you a seat at my table. I'm guessing you know there's more, don't you? Of course you do.

For those who know their scriptures, you will be aware that Ben and Jai's ancestors, Benjamin and Joseph, were very close. Joseph however, was homosexual, he had no interest in his wives, so Benjamin became the surrogate father, providing Joseph with most of his heirs; the eldest was Joseph's but the rest were Benjamin's. And for the record, Jai is descended from one of Joseph's heirs and not Benjamin's. Anyway, I digress.

It was fine back then, because they were related, so it didn't matter if Joseph's children bore a telling resemblance to Benjamin. Likewise, it can't have escaped your notice that Ben here is quite beautiful, his features are undeniably striking and his skin, a deep olive colour. He looks nothing like the majority of his male clients, yet he has fathered many of their children. His ancestor is known to have fathered ten children, though his wives are scarcely mentioned, not even apocryphally. No prizes for guessing what happened to them. Ben must have at least doubled that, by now.

That's not enough though, Ben here couldn't father all these children if he used contraception. So, apart from fathering lots of little Ben bastards, he is a carrier of syphilis and HIV. He will never suffer himself, but the men and women he seduces will. So, you tell me, just how many have you sentenced to death? How many divorces, suicides and infanticides have you been responsible for?

I think it's time for Exhibits A and B, don't you, Sam? Our jurors need some evidence to be able to make an informed decision. They shouldn't just take my word for it.

And please, eat up, it's almost time for the next course—but first, the evidence."

Exhibit A. A selection of photos depicting those who had either been murdered by enraged partners or ashamed parents. The images were horrific: burned babies, decapitated lovers, children who had been forced to swallow the barrel of a gun. Exhibit B was more photos, this time of those who had taken their own lives.

"As you can see, cannibalism might have been easier to ... well, to swallow. Which leads me on to the next course. The palate cleanser."

# CHAPTER IX
## DANYL



*Junkie on the streets of Jerusalem. Homeless,
and given over to a life of crime.
Lives in the shadows, where he hears much
but remembers little.
Single.*

"Ah, we come to Danyl from the tribe of Dan. A tribe considered wicked from its very beginning.

By the way, thank you, daughters of Iblis, this looks fantastic. Tonight's palate cleanser is a Lucretia *le spécial du chef*, Poppy's Blood Orange Sorbet with a glass of traditional Green Fairy from the Mystical Apothecary. Please allow all the water to have dripped into the glass before drinking. One should never try to rush the louche, and as you can see, despite the presence of djinn and demon, we prefer the French ritual. We are heathens not peasants.

And so, to Danyl, the only one who is still Jewish, and lives in Israel, although your ancestor was born in the north of Canaan, which was known for being sinister and evil. And

Dan was biblically described as the black sheep of the family. There is a distinct irony in being the black sheep in a flock of black sheep. It is almost poetic don't you think?

So, what was this black sheep guilty of, that earned him such a title? He was definitely evil, but was he any worse than his brothers? Hell no! Like all his brothers, he was given a blessing from Jacob, his father. Dan's blessing was that he shall judge his people as one of the tribes of Israel, but that he shall also be a snake by the roadside, a viper along the path, that bites the horse's heels so that it rears up and its rider falls behind it.

Your ancestor was indeed both judgemental and a viper. As are you, are you not?"

All eyes, including Azrael's, fixed on Danyl, who found the gazes of all the daughters of Iblis particularly unsettling.

"Dan was an idolator who called upon Belial and prayed to shayāṭīn. But what are your false idols, Danyl? Ah yes, money and heroin. By the way, are you alright, do you need a fix? Of course you do, now I've mentioned it.

Daughters of Iblis, fetch Danyl the works, and get him the good stuff."

The daughters soon returned, with tourniquet, teaspoon, citric acid, syringe and the all-important bag.

"I'm not one to deprive a man of his ritual, so while Danyl sorts himself out I will continue with his story.

Danyl's parents died in a train crash when he was very young. The young Danyl was brought up by his paternal grandparents. He had a strict upbringing, attended synagogue, studied hard and was well and truly set on the right path. And then he met Asher at the Hebrew University of Jerusalem. Asher was a wild child who completely embraced the recreational use of cannabis and alcohol, and Danyl, who for the first time in his life was free to make his own choices, made the wrong choice. Asher was able to leave his partying days behind him when he left but for Danyl it was all just gateway drugs to class A substance abuse.

By the time he was 25, Danyl was married with a baby, alongside a very expensive drug habit. Like all drug addicts, he lost his job, struggled to pay the rent and feed his family, but always managed to feed his habit. Something had to change.

All drug addicts, without exception, are resourceful and will protect their habit at any cost. And the one thing in the way of his habit was his family. So, he began by feeding his wife small amounts of liquid morphine in her food, just enough for it to be present in the bloodstream. Over time he increased it, as before, not enough to arouse suspicion but enough for her to need it. She began to have headaches as it left her bloodstream, and attentive husband that he was, Danyl would get her a drink. Of course, instead of soluble headache tablets he would lace her a drink with, you guessed it, morphine.

Eventually she became ill—not hospital ill, more like flu—enough to be uncomfortable. That was your opportunity to be free, wasn't it Danyl? All you needed was a healthy overdose of morphine followed by a shot of street heroin.

He lifted the … no, wait. Watch for yourselves. Samael, exhibit A, if you please."

They all watched the video footage as Danyl took his baby son out of his crib and lay him on the bed beside his dying mother. He then injected his son and rolled his wife onto the baby—both drugged and seemingly unaware of the inevitability of the situation. Danyl left the room and an eerie silence loomed over mother and son, as they drew their last breaths.

The coroner recorded it as death by misadventure. Clearly the mother also had a drug problem. Shortly after the funeral, Danyl was evicted and has lived on the streets ever since.

All that said, he may be a drug addict, but he is not stupid. He lives in the shadows close enough to the large prestigious hotels. Close enough to take note of the comings and goings. Close enough to see bosses and secretaries making the most of a weekend away from their spouses. Close enough to get enough dirt on people to blackmail them. And a street rat can always tell a streetwalker from a call girl, or a wife from a mistress, so Danyl here always knows who to target. I mean, there is no point in targeting a streetwalker, now is there? But the men who pay them, that's a different matter.

They always pay, usually quite handsomely, and when they stop paying, well, you know, don't you, Danyl? After all, husbands and wives can only skim so much off a joint account before their spouses become suspicious. And as we all know, some have hotter tempers than others. Exhibit B please, Sam."

A selection of crime scene photos was handed to the guests, some murder and some suicide. All, like his wife and son, were dead, and all for the price of a fix.

# CHAPTER X
## GERRY

*Security guard and boxing coach from New York.*
*Popular with his peers and highly respected by those younger than him.*
*Short marriages to three wives. Three children; two boys, one girl.*

"Allow me to delight you with our second main course: Blood Sausage with Angel Hair Pasta, drizzled with extra virgin olive oil, and washed down with a Bloody Mary Punch.

And of course, Gerald. Or Gerry, as he prefers, is descended from the tribe of Gad. Gad was the strongest of the twelve brothers and also the cruellest. He had a quick temper and murdered several of his concubines and their children, at times quite brutally. Joseph was afraid of him and denied him in Egypt, as he knew Pharaoh would be impressed by Gad's strength and want him as a bodyguard, possibly even as a lover. Either way, Joseph's relationship with Pharaoh, and his Egyptian status would have been greatly affected.

Gerry here, is equally strong with a violent nature, too aggressive at times, as was his upbringing. He was brought up in East Harlem. His father was a violent drunk and a paedophile, and let's just say the apple doesn't fall far from the tree. His mother, like the young Gerry, was both physically and sexually abused until eventually she found the courage to have his father arrested and charged. Gerry's father suffered an ironic fate; raped and beaten to death by some of the other prisoners.

These days Gerry lives in Midtown, New York, where he works nights as a security guard, and part time—mostly weekends—as a boxing coach.

The nights can be long and lonely, but don't be fooled, Gerry here has had his fair share of women. Been married three times, had several kids too: two boys and one girl. He doesn't see them though.

His first wife, Jane—plain Jane, as he called her—was the mother of his two eldest sons, and the first to discover just how like his father he was. However, unlike his mother, she found the courage to leave him before her boys suffered.

Jane was rapidly followed by Alex. Now there was a woman. She was, as they say, drop dead gorgeous. Alex was a model, earned good money and gave it all up for Gerry here. Alex absolutely doted on him, pandered to his every need. A threesome? Yes, my love. Being tied up and slapped? Why, certainly dear. Golden shower? Well, I'll try anything once. But where is the fun in that, eh Gerry? And so, what was your final fetish? Oh yes, I recall— snuff.

Alex had a daughter, a baby at the time of her mother's death. Where is she now? Yes, you guessed it, she's buried with her mother. The police never found them, but *we* know exactly where they are.

And then came Mary. She was sweet. Yes, sweet is the best description of her. Not as beautiful as Alex but attractive by any standard. She loved Gerry here, perhaps even more so than the others. She was smart, too; could have had everything but for one mistake. You see, Mary was a lawyer. I told you she was smart. Smart enough to keep her husband out of trouble when he got into an unauthorised fight at the boxing club with one of the other coaches. I doubt Gerry here can even remember what it was over now."

Gerry glared at Azrael. He viewed himself as a man not to be trifled with, and yet Azrael was treating him like a cat toying with a mouse. Of course, he knew what the fight was about.

"Mary. It was about Mary," Gerry snapped, before Azrael got the chance to speak.

Azrael nodded.

"Yes, it was about Mary. Beat the guy to within an inch of his life. He was in intensive care for several months. Obviously, Gerry was arrested and somehow Mary got him out of jail and all charges were dropped. Impressive lady. And I'm sure you are wondering how this lady caused such a fight in the first place. You would think the guy must have raped her, or something.

On the night in question, Mary had come down to the club to meet Gerry after training. As they had turned to leave, the man had said she had a nice arse. Most people would just take it as a compliment. Not Gerry. You would also think that Mary would have left him, but no.

It was early one evening, when Gerry was getting ready for work, that Mary returned home late from the office. She was smiling and a little too happy, I guess. Why the smile? Well, as it happened, she had been given a promotion. I mean, if you can get someone like Gerry here off, then you are an asset worth keeping hold of. That wasn't all of it, the pay rise was insane. Too insane apparently; clearly, she must have done something *extra* to warrant such a reward.

An inevitable argument ensued, and Mary tried desperately hard to maintain her innocence, but to no avail. So, Gerry here, decided to beat a confession out of her. Samael, exhibit A please."

Exhibit A was a video, which began with Gerry twisting Mary's arm. The twisting became harder and harder, and she screamed, tears flooding down her cheeks. Her arm finally gave way and snapped, and the fight ended, although they could see that Mary had no fight left in her long before this point. The video ended with him stamping on his wife's face as her lifeless body lay in a pool of her own blood.

"Mary currently resides in a compact little spot close to Alex and her daughter, her battered corpse, as yet undiscovered by the NYPD."

# CHAPTER XI
## ISOBELLA

*Raised in Vatican City, where she still resides.*
*Graduated from university with honours.*
*Works as a highly paid teacher at the Vatican,*
*in a job created especially for her.*

"And so, we reach the cheese course. I believe on tonight's cheese board is Byaslag, Stinking Bishop, Dirt lover and an obligatory blue veined cheese— always a favourite. This will be accompanied by a selection of chutney and a side order of Pigs in Shrouds, which incidentally are the same as Pigs in Blankcts, just with a more sinister name. This will be served with a bottle of the finest sacramental wine.

*Ah, fair Isobella,*
*such beauty and such grace,*
*never did exist,*
*except in my Isobella's face.*

Do you like that, Isobella? Of course you do, and your face is undeniably beautiful, but your character—well, that's another matter.

A descendant of the Tribe of Issachar. Your ancestor was a scholar who knew his scriptures well and had been brought up to obey and worship Yahweh as the one true god. The god of his father, and his father before him, and so on. Issachar's crime was the worshipping of *false* gods—the Egyptian gods—in exchange for wealth. You and he are alike in many ways, but you are far more mercenary.

Isobella grew up in the Vatican City. Her family were devout Catholics, and she grew up learning the bible inside out but yet something was always missing. Her parents died in a traffic accident back in 2013, when she was 20. This had a huge impact on the young Isobella, leaving a massive gap in her life. She initially worked through her grief by studying hard and striving towards that which she knew would have made them proud. She achieved it too, graduated with honours and got a good job within the Vatican.

This job was created purely for Isobella. Why? You may well ask. Perhaps there was more to her parents' untimely death, and this was yet another cover-up job by the Holy See. Or perhaps Isobella was just the right breed of Catholic for the job.

As for the job, well, that involved coaching prospective altar boys and nuns—effectively grooming them, by any other name. How many cloistered nuns and altar boys did she train to be abused? I believe the total number was twenty-three, all of them children.

This, however, is not where it ends. Isobella worked 5 days a week, but in the evenings, she topped up an already substantial income by soliciting on the streets of Rome.

Of course, prostitution itself is not the crime, certainly not to us. Hell, you provide a valuable service. At least in my book you do. Prostitution alone would never get you a dinner invite from me, not even from *your* god. No, it's grooming vulnerable young boys and young women, some of whom were barely women—that's your crime!

And truthfully, that would be enough to get my attention, but when you add it to your chosen method of birth control, well, voilà!

You see, Isobella here is Catholic enough not to use

preventative measures, and of course, when no precautions are taken, pregnancy is inevitable. Again, neither unmarried mothers, nor abortions are crimes. We're angels, demons and shayāṭīns, not monsters!

Just for the record, Isobella has had 12 abortions to date. The taking of a life in desperate and unfortunate circumstances is understandable. The taking of twelve lives to feed your bank account, well, that's different.

So, for the record, exhibits A and B please, Samael."

The court listened to the screams of young nuns and altar boys being deflowered. And were presented with images of aborted foetuses and those boys and girls for whom the abuse was just too much, and death more welcoming. All were labelled with how much she had earned from them.

"Oh Isobella, such a beautiful face, but a vile and wretched soul. Like I said, just the right breed of Catholic!"

# CHAPTER XII
## NATHAN

*Firefighter from New York.*
*In line for promotion since saving a child's life*
*while risking his own.*
*Married with a stepdaughter.*

"Oh, sweet Nathan, for you a dessert course. Something sweet for the man who helps so many: a good old-fashioned Banana Split. Can't beat the classics. This, I feel, would be best served with a Flaming Backdraft.

Let's set the night ablaze and ignite the soul! What do you say? Nothing, huh? Cat got your tongue?"

The guests remained silent.

Nathan looked at Azrael as if he were about to speak but had thought better of it.

"Descended from the Tribal leader, Naphtali, also known as the Hind, because he could run so fast. Incidentally, and in case you didn't know, being named for such an ability is biblical for coward. Naphtali never defended his family, his honour, or his tribe. He left his wives to be burned to death rather than fighting to save them. Instead, he took his sons and ran to Egypt seeking sanctuary.

Nathan, however, is a New York fire fighter. A city on fire at the best of times. It is therefore reasonable to assume he risks his life on a daily basis. He does, and it would seem that for such bravery he received a medal and a promotion for saving a young girl's life, a year ago. Very heroically too, I might add. Risked his own life and was even in hospital for a couple of weeks. I assume his wife and stepdaughter must be very proud.

Oh yes, he has no children of his own, and how honourable to take on another man's child. Nathan is an honourable man. But is he though?

Here are some little known facts about the heroic Nathan. He did not save that girl. Nathan, as always, was nowhere near the danger zone, he only ever goes a safe distance into a burning building. So, who did save her you ask? Good question. And blow me down with an angel's feather, it was only one of his co-workers. Obviously a braver one than Nathan.

So, how come his colleague didn't get the medal instead of

Nathan? Let me show you. Exhibit A please, Samael.”

The film showed Nathan at a safe distance from the blaze, hiding in the shadows, presumably hoping he wouldn't be noticed. He was obscured from his colleague's view as he ran past carrying a small girl, who appeared to be  slipping in and out of consciousness. Nathan didn't waste a second, he seized the nearest heavy object and knocked his colleague to the floor, grabbed the girl and hid her where he had been a few seconds earlier. He then dragged his colleague back into the burning building, returned to the girl and carried her heroically out of the building. Without a shadow of a doubt the whole thing was very cleverly executed.

“As you can see, his colleague died equally heroically in the line of duty.”

Azrael paused for a moment, and stared directly at Nathan, who was doing his best not to make eye contact.

“It may be easier to live with yourself when you know the family is being looked after, but the reality is, you deprived two small children of their father. And there is no denying the impact your actions would have had on his family. But hey, they knew the risks, I mean the guy was a firefighter, after all.”

At this point Azrael returned to addressing the room.

“Nathan was an absolute hero of course; saved that girl, snatched her from the jaws of death. I mean, a few more minutes and she wouldn’t have made it.

Now, here’s the real fun fact. The fires where Nathan bravely earned his salary by hiding in the shadows, and the one where he heroically risked his life to save that girl by killing the man who had been saving her ... all of them were started by him.” Azrael peered around the room at the look of shock on the faces of his guests.

“And even better, he’s always got away with it ... until now of course.”

# CHAPTER XIII
## ZACK

*Bisexual cult leader from Virginia. Both parents deceased—difficult relationship with his father. Was investigated by the IRS but no tax fraud discovered.*

"And so, we come to the mignardise course. Our final course. Tonight, we have Cry-Baby Biscuits with Blood Orange Segments, accompanied by a cup of Dead-Eye Coffee. Please enjoy."

Azrael waved his hand in a sweeping gesture before taking a sip of Dead-Eye.

"Please, allow me to introduce our final guest, last but never least, Zack.

Zack's ancestor was Zebulun, a god-fearing and pious man with a dark side. He conspired with his brethren against their brother, Joseph, which was gutless of him, as like Joseph, Zebulun had an eye for the boys. This of course is no crime, as you by now know, but laziness is. Zebulun was idle—bone idle. He spent his days flirting with other members of the tribe, and his wife and children went hungry. Very hungry. They would have starved to death but for Naphtali and Judah helping them.

And so to Zack, you may recognise his face from the papers—a cult leader from Virginia. He was investigated a while back for allegations of tax fraud, but like the rest of you, came out of that shit-show smelling of roses. Was he guilty of tax fraud? Amazingly not, and as long as the I.R.S. are happy, everything else is OK.

So, let me tell you about Zack. He was raised on his daddy's small ranch in Virginia. Life was pretty good there; a lot of space for a kid and his dog to run around, home cooked meals, and a doting father. What more could a child want? Nothing. It was idyllic and to some extent, comfortably predictable.

His family worked hard all week, sold produce at the market on Saturdays and went to church on Sundays. They were respected, and well-liked by everyone, including those they employed.

His daddy's ranch was small and most of what needed doing could be considered chores. They had a small herd of cattle, which, for the most part, he and Zack could manage. The farmhouse was large, too large really but nonetheless Zack's mother kept it clean and tidy. She tended the small orchard and vegetable garden as well as churning butter and cheese to sell at market.

During the breeding season, Zack's father would take on a couple of hired hands to help out. Because Daddy believed in treating his staff well, they always shared the family's home throughout the summer months.

One summer, when Zack was 17-years-old, his daddy noticed Zack was showing, as he put it, an unhealthy interest in a young hand. He hoped that suggesting his son seek guidance from the lord would be an end to it. It wasn't. Sexuality is not something so easily controlled, and several towns in Virginia had, shall we say, an aversion to same sex couples—an aversion with a passion.

Zack's home town was one of the last places on earth a young homosexual wanted to be. The local community were prejudiced, if not fiercely bigoted. Of course, Zack's daddy loved his son, but only as long as he was straight.

It wasn't till the following summer that Zack's father caught him kissing the new hand. That was the last time Zack saw his family alive. He was banished from the ranch with the strong suggestion that, for his own safety, he leave Virginia all together.

Zack's mother died a couple of years later. Cancer ate away at her. That, and a broken heart. Zack didn't go home for the funeral, and he resented his father even more for that.

When Zack was 30, news came of his daddy's death, and the ranch was his. That was when he moved back to Virginia. The last time he saw his daddy was just before they closed the lid.

That idyllic childhood was long forgotten and had been replaced with resentment and bitterness, and over the years this had grown into hatred. He requested that his father be buried on the ranch so he could visit his grave every day. He did, but only to urinate or defecate on it."

All eyes fell on Zack and several guests curled their lips in disgust.

"Oh, look at you all, such pillars of the community, so far that is his worst crime. Can you all say the same?" Azrael's laughter echoed around the room.

"Such a loving son." Samael offered, as he passed around images of Zack defecating on his father's grave.

"Indeed," Azrael continued. "These are not really evidence of anything," he swept his hand across the photos littered around the table. "They are merely for our amusement. Once Zack had moved back into the ranch, he considered ways to *honour* his daddy's memory. So, he sold the precious livestock, and bought a couple of cows for milking, some laying hens, corn and vegetable seeds. He was going to become self-sufficient. He would build high fences and keep the world out. On his ranch—in his world—there would be no sexual taboos. No prejudice.

He could not do this alone. Phase one, establish a reason people will help you, apart from paying them. Better still, get them to pay you.

Zack had grown up with small town mentality, so although the laws may have changed, he doubted people's attitudes had. The other thing he knew was what made members of the LGBTQ communities tick—he knew their fears and their desires, *his people*.

One of the big issues, he knew, was the church vs homosexuality. The priesthood, as we know, has never had a problem with altar boys, but these were southern Baptists, and the god of the south was a very different god to the one in Europe—different even to the god of the northern United States.

Zack found those desperate to be accepted, desperate to feel safe and desperate to believe their god did not view them as sinners. Zack offered hope to all those society had shunned, at his newly named commune, New Babylon.

In the beginning there were twelve members of New Babylon but word travels fast and proselytizing is a gift from God. New members signed their worldly goods over to Zack and he used it to build more living accommodation.

New Babylon was self-sufficient, everybody, whether man, woman or child, worked. The commune ran like clockwork. Every evening Zack would preach his version of god's holy word and of course, in exchange for all this love and acceptance, his god made demands of his congregation. These included signing over all your wealth to the community, giving yourself over to God via his prophet—completely. In case you are in any doubt, this meant sleeping with Zack.

Are these sins enough to get my attention? Of course not. In fact, most of tonight's staff would probably give him a pat on the back. So, there has to be more to it.

Zack was never gay, he was bisexual—and promiscuous.

Ultimately, this led to the births of children, and the under-fives were useless, they couldn't work—oh yes, he had 5-year-olds working. The under-fives proved, however, to be a drain on resources and so *God* decreed that they be *offered* to him, and they would be among the *heavenly host.* They were starved to death and then burned on a bonfire.

Eventually, this became the fate of any who did not, or could not, pull their weight. Those who became injured while working were effectively left to die of starvation in locked outhouses that stank of shit and piss. The sounds of children and adults crying, separated from those they loved, knowing their death was inevitable. But when their cries became unbearable, they were burned alive. How did you put it? Ah yes, I remember.

*God has heard your cries, he knows your suffering, and in his mercy, has chosen to end your suffering now.*

Exhibit B please, Samael."

Samael ran the video of the children left to die—many of which were Zack's own children—and those burned alive.

# DEFENCE

# CHAPTER XIV
## RUBY

"Daughters of Iblis, some more Dead-Eye coffee if you please. It really is rather good, isn't it?"

The shayāṭīn placed a large pot in the centre of the table.

"And so, to your defences. Not that any of you have one, but I'm nothing, if not reasonable. Please, anybody? Ruby? Yes, Ruby, let's start with you."

Ruby glared at him.

"You, and everyone else here, already know what my childhood was like. You made sure everyone knew," she hissed at him. "I was a frightened little girl, left alone in a cold dark world. How did you expect me to turn out? I had no moral upbringing and no love. I was—am—a very damaged little girl. Well, I may not be so little these days, but I am still very damaged. Years of abuse does that to you, and I spent my formative years as my mother's punch bag. She would come home drunk and accuse me of driving my father away.

I recall, all too vividly, how she would hit me with an old metal serving spoon. I'm not even sure why she owned it, it's not as if she ever cooked anything. I can still feel the metal hitting my skin and I go to bed each night with the words *useless little slut*, her words, echoing around inside my head. I know what I did was wrong. With hindsight I would do things very differently. In fact, if I get the opportunity to walk out of here, I will do my utmost to make a positive difference."

"Are those crocodile tears, Ruby?" Danyl rasped, the heroin and alcohol clearly having got more control over him than common sense.

"SILENCE!" Azrael's voice thundered. "It is not for you to question. If I were any of you, I would worry about my own defence, not Ruby's."

# CHAPTER XV
## LEWIS

"I believe Lewis has something to offer. Do you not?"

Lewis shifted uncomfortably in his seat.

"Shooting those children was a mercy killing. They would have died alone out there, probably would have starved to death."

"Even if that were true, which it isn't, why mutilate their little bodies? And your family? The ones you stoned to death, were they going to starve to death too?"

Lewis looked around the room.

"I have no suitable defence, just hollow excuses."

"Hollow excuses are a start."

"My childhood, as you said, was fairly typical for the time. My parents worked hard, and I spent a lot of time at my grandmother's. I only had one grandparent you see. My mum's mum. She doted on me and I on her.

Sadly, she died when I was 12-years-old. I was with her at the time— she had a heart attack. It was horrific to watch. I could see she was in pain and I was devasted. I called the ambulance but by the time they reached her she was gone. I never wanted anyone to suffer like that. I became fascinated by death. I killed rats to see how fast they would die. Stoning can be a very quick death when executed correctly.

Death is horrific, the idea of going through a painful death terrifies me. In the Gulf, death reached a whole new level of suffering. The battlefield is no place for the faint-hearted.

Those two children, I knew they could suffer a lot worse than being shot. Honestly, out there, orphaned children don't fare well. They are either exploited by predators or trained in combat: carrying guns, or worse, explosives, or they are prey. Those who are prey fare worse, as sex toys or slaves. For these children death is a mercy.

As to why I mutilated them. Initially I told myself to make them look as though they had been carrying explosives. But that excuse carries no weight when I look at my wife and children.

That night still haunts me, I was angry. I had lost my job and felt useless. My wife was drunk and taunting me. She could be a bitch at times, especially with a drink inside her. We were having some building work done and I picked up a brick. All those years of throwing stones at rats, I knew exactly how to kill her with one blow. She died instantly but I continued hitting her—I was angry, angry as hell. Then I remembered the children. I knew I couldn't cope with them alone, so I killed them too. I think I only continued my frenzied attack through frustration. I was hurt and angry and worse still, now I was alone.

I sorely regret my actions, always have, and I believe if I get to leave here, I will turn myself in and let them be laid to rest properly."

Azrael nodded. It was not clear to the others whether he believed Lewis but he was at least willing to acknowledge his defence.

# CHAPTER XVI
## ZACK

"I think most of us around this table are sorry. I know I am when I look back at it all. Seeing, the pictures and hearing the screams—such cruelty and horrors I inflicted, and yet somehow, I had convinced myself I was being merciful—"

"Seriously Zack! God's work? You believed that did you?" Simon glared at Zack as though it was him, not Azrael, who was in charge. "Honestly? You were a murderous sociopath. How can that possibly be God's work? God is about life, not burning people alive—"

"And we have all seen your version of life, haven't we Simon. For fuck's sake. Are you really in any position to judge? Cos from where I'm sitting, none of us are!"

"Ssshh," Azrael soothed. "Please, Zack, continue."

"Well," he began, taking a sip of Dead-Eye, "when I look back at everything, I can't help but wonder how things might have been different, had my father been more accepting of me. I also wonder if perhaps he may have been a little more like me than was comfortable. His era was less accepting than mine, especially in small town Virginia.

I was angry and resentful towards my father, and to some extent my mother. After all she didn't stand up to him. She just stood there and watched me leave, without so much as a hug.

When I returned, my hatred had grown towards him, and I intended to use his precious ranch to provide a safe haven for members of the LGBTQ. I did not believe God hated us for our sexuality. We were, after all, still his children. But power can be a dangerous mistress."

"Or master," interjected one of the daughters of Iblis.

"Indeed," Zack continued. "You see, those who are born with power know how to wield it without corruption. It is those who have never had power that are the most dangerous: fascist dictators, war lords, and idiots like me.

I was easily seduced by my newly found power. People were

following me, hanging on my every word, throwing money and themselves at me. Everyone wanted to sleep with me, and I began to believe the hype. The more they gave me, the more they worshipped me, the more I pushed it.

We could have fed those babies. Despite my insanity, we were a thriving commune. But I believed all the propaganda. I convinced myself I was doing God's will, that in some way I was his chosen one. I can see now how wrong that was. I would do it all so differently now, but I accept I may never get the chance to put things right."

# CHAPTER XVII
## NATHAN

"Now, let me see." Azrael poured himself another coffee and glanced casually around the room. "What about you, Nathan?"

Nathan sighed, as though he were carrying the weight of the world.

"You know, you never mentioned my childhood. Why is that?"

"I thought I'd leave you to tell us about it."

Nathan took a deep breath, or perhaps it was another sigh, and began to speak slowly and softly.

"I was brought up by my father. My mother died in a fire at the salon she worked in, when I was only young. My father never remarried, although he had several girlfriends, none became my stepmother. A few lingered around the periphery and became like aunties. One I was quite close to—Hannah. She was lovely and we spent a lot of time together. As a teenager I secretly had a bit of a thing for her, but she was much older, and nothing ever came of it.

I guess to some extent I was a bit of a mummy's boy, and although my dad tried to toughen me up, it never really happened. I remained a bit of a wimp.

I joined the fire service, so other kids wouldn't lose parents, as I had always missed having a mother, but I wasn't brave enough. I wasn't really cut out for it, but I desperately wanted to make my father proud.

I can't remember exactly when I first started a fire, but I do remember it.

It had been really quiet, just small fires and the like. So, we had been working on a skeleton crew, which meant I hadn't earned much that month, and I had a wife and stepdaughter to provide for. That's when it occurred to me. We would earn good money for a decent blaze—an *all hands on* fire, so to speak. It worked, and the rest you know. I continued to hang back from the main fire and the rest is history."

"Thank you. What about you, Simon? No? Nothing? OK then,

Isobella perhaps? Or maybe, Andros?
Danyl?

# CHAPTER XVIII
## ISOBELLA

"I'd like to say something, if I may?"

"Of course, Isobella, be my guest."

"On reflection, and there is much to reflect upon, I can see the error of my ways. However, and I am in no way justifying my actions, I do truly believe, that my parents' death had more effect on me, than I thought possible.

You see, growing up, I was very close to my parents but especially my mother, and after her death I was lost. My life spiralled out of control, and I made some very poor choices.

I became easily manipulated by those in power, those who should have been helping me. My father was a commissioned officer in the Swiss Guard and my mother was a lawyer. I only remember living within Vatican City.

I'd like to believe that if I was given the opportunity, I would change my ways, but that may just be wishful thinking on my part.

You see I know I wasn't a little girl, and I wasn't stupid. I knew their deaths were suspicious. Nobody is short of money in Vatican City, and everybody living there is a devout and loyal Catholic. Their car wasn't some old banger that needed a good service, it was brand new. Nor were driving conditions bad that day. My father was only 45 and my mother had just turned 40. Life is supposed to begin then—not end.

I always suspected there was more to my parents' deaths, but I couldn't prove it. The Vatican is powerful, and I was vulnerable.

As for the drinking, the prostitution and abortions, well, I think that was just my way of rebelling. Enough alcohol can make you forget who you are, at least for a while, and believe me I wanted to forget. I knew the Catholic church had little problem with prostitution, after all, they have been ardent customers since St Peter. I was hurt. I hated all they represented, but I liked the money, yet still I wanted to make them pay, and abortion is something they would never accept.

I'd like to say that if I had my time over I would do things differently, but perhaps you are right, perhaps I am simply the right breed of Catholic monster."

"Is there nothing you would change? Do differently? This coffee is really good, is there any more?" Azrael nodded to the shayāṭīn, who returned moments later with more coffee.

"I would definitely reconsider my method of contraception, as you put it. As for the drinking and prostitution, I can't say for sure. I'd like to think I'd stop, but maybe I'm more damaged than I think."

"What about that high-paid grooming job? There's rich pickings to be made there, and as you said you do like money."

"I do, but I think with hindsight I would leave it and the Vatican far behind. Although ..."

"I'm listening." Not only was Azrael listening, a demon and three shayāṭīn edged closer, as their interest, too, was piqued.

"Well, say I continued my job but taught a different skillset. Now that they have created this job, they aren't going to let it go, they will just find another vulnerable soul who is the *right breed of Catholic.*

What if, instead, I let them pay me but taught these youngsters how not to take their final vows? I wouldn't get away with it for long, but perhaps long enough to save a few of them, and of course I would encourage them to expose those involved. I could then support their claims, hopefully get witness protection and my job would cease to exist—they would have no choice."

Isobella stared directly at Azrael, Samael and the daughters of Iblis, who in turn looked at each other.

"Well, what do you think?" The response was a silence, that hung heavily above her, almost crushing her soul.

Eventually Azrael spoke.

"I think you really are just the right breed of Catholic."

# CHAPTER XIX
## DANYL

"Asher."

"What's that Danyl?"

"Asher, Asher!" he screamed. "Asher was to blame. He introduced me to drugs. It was his fault. All his fault."

"Was it? Was it really? Was it Asher who made you kill your wife and baby son? Was it Asher who blackmailed all those people? No. It was you. Honestly Danyl, defend yourself, don't just point your fingers at others, that is not the way it is done here."

Danyl hung his head. Azrael was right there was no one to blame but himself.

"I was a good Jewish boy. I loved my grandparents, studied my scriptures and I had a bright future ahead of me, that is until I met Asher.

Asher was my age and came from a similar background, although his parents were still alive. They were older, and like my grandparents, they were strict but where I had obeyed my grandparents, Asher had rebelled against his upbringing. I hadn't even considered such a thing, but once I dipped my toe in the waters of rebellion, I knew I was lost. Of course, back then I could have stopped but I wasn't aware there would be a day when I couldn't.

In the beginning it was fun. Asher and I partied our way through university. By the time we graduated from university, we had already graduated from hashish to heroin. We spent the last year of Uni thinking we were the crème de la crème. We were the elite, we could afford heroin. Well, Asher could. As soon as we graduated, his parents whisked him away and I was left alone with a very expensive drug habit, and not so well-off grandparents.

My grandfather recognised the signs of heroin addiction instantly. Apparently my father had developed a problem with prescription opioids following surgery to remove a tumour in his bladder, hence him no longer driving. Had he been OK to drive, my parents wouldn't have been on that ill-fated train.

I was given three opportunities by my grandparents to get help before they threw me out. I hated them for abandoning me. I hated Asher for introducing me. I hated the world for rejecting me. But most of all, I hated me for allowing myself to be seduced by the notion of rebellion. What was I even rebelling against? Those who loved me? Yahweh? Society? Whatever it was, it doesn't much matter now.

My grandfather died shortly after he threw me out. His heart gave out. According to my grandmother, he was old and these things happen, but I suspect I was the final straw—my father and now me.

My grandmother let me move back home on the proviso I cleaned up. She had even found me a wife from a good family. She viewed this as an opportunity to put things right—to put myself right. I think a part of me knew this would be a disaster, but I went along with it.

It was easy to convince her that I was clean because she so desperately wanted it to be true. But I wasn't, and I had no job beyond thieving. I was a market-place pick-pocket. Feeding a habit and a wife this way was bad enough, but when my son was born, I knew I could not provide for them.

So, I stole the opioids still at my grandparents' house, left over from my father all those years ago, and fed them slowly to my wife. I half expected them to either not work or kill her outright, but they didn't. The rest you know.

I miss her, and if I'm honest, I had wanted a wife and a son, I was just weak and couldn't fight my addiction. Blackmailing rich people cheating on their husbands and wives was lucrative and merely provided a means to numb the pain of all I had lost, and all I have become.

I know that I don't deserve to walk out of here, but if by some miracle I do, then I will seek spiritual help from Yahweh and physical help from a doctor."

Azrael laughed.

"If you walk out of here, I can assure you it will not be the result of a miracle."

# CHAPTER XX
## GERRY

Gerry, do you have anything to bring to the table? Any defence for beating your wife to death?

"She wasn't all sweetness and light you know. Mary had a dark side. They all did. Women can be very cruel at times—hurtful—and I do have feelings. I don't mean to lose my temper, it's just, well it just happens sometimes."

"Really? That's all you have? A bunch of empty excuses—nothing else?"

"They aren't just excuses. I honestly am very sorry for my actions."

Azrael looked deep into Gerry's eyes.

"You had three wives, did you not?"

Gerry sighed and nodded his head. "Jane was lovely. I only ever called her plain Jane affectionately, and we were fine for a while. Long enough to have two children. I remember the night before she left, I was drunk—very drunk, and she started complaining about how I spent all our money on booze. She was really angry, started hitting me and scratching me. She had long nails, see, I still bear the marks." Gerry lifted his shirt to reveal his scars.

"Jeez, it looks as though you got in a fight with a lion," Julian thoughtlessly blurted out. "I mean, what the fuck?"

Azrael scowled at Julian, raised his finger to his lips, before gesturing to Gerry to lower his shirt and continue.

"I sobered up pretty quick but I was angry and in pain. There was a fair amount of my blood dripping on the lounge carpet. I lost my temper and punched her several times before I raped her. Neither of us deserved each other that night and she was right to leave. In the end, I was my father's son.

And yes, I did push Alex sexually. She was so damned compliant—it was all too easy. There was nothing she wouldn't do, I honestly thought she was a masochist, and you cannot rape a woman who lets you. I just needed her to say no sometimes. I was bored, and so yes, in the end my sexual appetite and temper got the better of me. As for her baby, I couldn't have looked after her, and I was still hyped up from killing her mother. Looking back, it was blind rage, so much so, it almost seems like a dream."

"I'm sure you've told yourself that on many occasions. The reality is far more horrific though, isn't it?"

Gerry winced; he knew Azrael was right.

"It wasn't quite the same with Mary." Gerry continued. "Like I said, she could say some really hurtful things at times, although she didn't deserve the beating I gave her. The night she died she was late home, and tipsy with a big smile. When she told me about her pay rise, I assumed it was for services rendered, so to speak. I accused her of all sorts and she began to cry—sobbed like a little baby she did. She stopped, all of a sudden, sniffed a bit and screamed at me that I was a controlling, heartless, manipulative psychopath. She didn't stop there though—oh no. She added that I had a small mind and an even smaller dick. That's when I saw red.

I regret my actions, of course I do, and I have no idea how much is nature and how much is nurture. Or indeed, at times, how much is alcohol.

I guess I, too, may live out my days in prison, or meet the same fate as my father, and all that is assuming I even get to leave here."

"Indeed, one cannot make any assumptions on nights such as these."

# CHAPTER XXI
## BEN

"Ah Ben, the ravenous little wolf with whom one night is truly a lethal injection. Your defence, please."

Ben looked across at Azrael wondering if his introduction had a hint of affection in it, or if, as he suspected, he was just deluding himself—clutching at straws. Whatever it was, it at least felt more comfortable than his earlier introduction.

"I am, as our host informed you, the real deal when it comes to seeing the future. And, as also stated, I have what appears to be a sex addiction, as they say. Of course, I have sought treatment for this, but it always involves will power, and I can resist anything except temptation.

It took a while before I realised I carried  syphilis and HIV. No one had ever told me, but it turns out I was born with syphilis. My mother was never ill. She, like me, was just a carrier but my father had been less than impressed when he'd not only contracted a dose but also found out that he had a bastard child on the way. I never met my father. Apparently, he gave my pregnant mother a good hiding and was never seen again. My uncle said it was a miracle she didn't lose the baby, and well here I am—a pox ridden little miracle.

Also, like our host told you, no one goes to a fortune teller when life is going great, which makes it easy to take advantage. I'm not sure when I contracted HIV, but I do remember the first time I passed it on. It was a genuine accident, and I was mortified. Truth to tell, I had grown incredibly callous, having taken a few beatings from irate husbands and boyfriends for passing on syph. Even had a couple of women get quite handsy too. But, let's face it, syph is curable, only a real idiot wouldn't get treated. But HIV, well, that's a whole other matter.

I honestly didn't know I had it. I already had several *Ben bastards* out there, and just as many irate fathers and mothers. The only ones who weren't angry were a couple of lesbian ladies who were desperate for a child. For the most part, the mothers of my children loved their babies. Not all, but most.

Anyway, I digress. Let me return to the first time I passed on HIV. A very famous author, Tom Grimes, had come to see me after his boyfriend had left him a couple of months previous. It turned out that he had recently attempted suicide too. He couldn't feel much lower.

He was still young and very beautiful, and I wanted him desperately. That's the trouble, my desperate longing. Anyway, it didn't take too much to convince him to sleep with me. His future looked good, he looked set for the big time and would have no money worries. He seemed happy with that, or at least happier, and don't get me wrong I didn't lie, I just didn't tell him everything.

I saw him in the street a couple of years later, he had written a show that was opening in the West End, but he didn't look well. He didn't see me. Later that year I read of his death from AIDS.

Initially I was worried that I may have contracted it, so I got tested. I had contracted it, but not from him. I read of another former lover's death from that dreaded disease. That's when it dawned on me that I was the one who had passed it to Tom. I suppose I should have seen it coming, the gift of foresight and all that, but I guess I just wasn't looking.

However much it upset me, it didn't stop me and I honestly have no idea how many deaths I have caused. More than I care to think about, that's for sure.

Everyone else has said that they would try to change their ways. I am weak, I know that, but I guess at the very least I would use contraception. I'm not sure I'm strong enough to totally mend my ways but I like to think I would try."

Azrael scanned the room.

"Julian, your turn."

It was as if Ben had never spoken.

# CHAPTER XXII
## JULIAN

"I'm not sure what you want me to say. I grew up a *half-cast queer boy,* as my dad's friends put it, surrounded by hookers and those who frequented gin joints, strip clubs, and gay bars. I was *mischlingskinder* in a world of sleaze.

My father had more whores than hot dinners, and my mother sang for the money he used to pay for his whores. I didn't stand a chance. What would I do differently? Ideally, I'd start with different parents.

Don't get me wrong, I know the crimes I'm guilty of are horrific. I've behaved like a complete cunt and have no excuse for any of it. The trouble is it was all too easy. And more importantly, it was easy money.

Sadly, Azrael is right, I had learned to detach myself from the whole thing. Hookers, rent boys—these weren't people as such, they were trinkets. Expensive trinkets, but trinkets, nonetheless. They adorned their customers in the same way strippers adorned their stages, in the same way that trinkets briefly adorn the wearer. They were all mere trifles, dalliances, and their lives were cheap and disposable.

I know I sound cruel; I see Ruby and Isobella both cringing, but deep down they know I'm right. The sex industry is just that—an industry. People are hired and fired, and all too often used and discarded. They break or grow old much too quickly. Whores have a short shelf life, as do strippers. No one wants to see their grandmother take her clothes off.

Looking at the exhibits, I can't be anything else but ashamed and sorry. Sorry I didn't take another path. Sorry I didn't make life easier for those I was allegedly responsible for. That's a joke—I wasn't even responsible for myself, how could I be? I used as much cocaine as I dished out. And all the while hiding my sexuality to make my dad proud.

I know I don't deserve to walk out of here, and I'm not sure what I would do differently, but I'd like to think I'd do something, however small, to make a positive difference to these people's lives. I guess, like Isobella, I could bring a lot of people to justice, assuming I can find the balls to do so.”

“And that’s your defence, is it? Interesting.”

“Look man, I get it, one of us is gonna die here tonight, and Lord knows I deserve to die. I can’t undo what I’ve done. And you know what, to some extent I imagine everyone in this room is sorry, but sorry doesn’t take away the guilt. I can only hope that if I get the chance to put some of it right, I have the bollocks to do so.”

“I see. Let’s see how sorry the rest of you are.”

# CHAPTER XXIII
## SIMON

"I'm not sure what I should say really. I mean, I believe that all life is precious, especially new life."

"Oh, indeed, without a shadow of a doubt that newborn baby is, by far, the best of humanity. Sin free, guilt free—just think, you were all like that once. Tiny, precious, bundles of purity, as close to divine as it gets.

*In divine love all life is born,*
*Through divine love all life is born,*
*For divine love is all life born."*

"Exactly, and all I have tried to do is save that precious new life. I cannot see how that is a crime.

I am the first to admit it doesn't always go according to plan, but I'm sure God forgives any errors in judgement I may have made in my attempts to do his bidding. I know I have been a bit, well, negligent at times, but on the whole I am a good doctor and I try to be a good man.

And the young girl you mentioned earlier, well, I'm sorry for that. It was unfortunate but there was nothing I could do."

"You mean, there was nothing you were willing to do. There's a difference."

"I mean there was nothing I could do, it was her time to go."

Azrael tapped his fingers on the table. "I need more Dead-Eye. Tell me, Simon, is there nothing you regret—nothing you would do differently."

"To atone for that which you call my sins? God is my judge, not you. You are merely an angel, at least that is assuming you are who you say you are."

Everybody looked at Simon, trying to decide if he was right, brave, or mad. Within seconds, the unholy sound of demon and shayāṭīn laughing hysterically echoed around the room like nails on a blackboard.

"SILENCE!" screamed Azrael. "Enough. Fetch more coffee, and cognac, Henri IV Dudognon Heritage, please. Now let us move on—it is getting late."

# CHAPTER XXIV

## ANDROS

"Eeny, meeny, miny, Andros! Yes, let's hear Andros's version of events. Such complex strategies."

Andros puffed out his cheeks and blew.

"What can I possibly say that will make any difference? Do I regret it? Yes and no. I have precious few regrets where Damian or Daphne are concerned."

"Please elaborate." Azrael offered, while Samael poured everyone, including himself and the daughters of Iblis, a glass of ridiculously expensive cognac.

"Alex would have looked after the place and done as good a job as any of us—better probably. But rightly or wrongly, I wanted the place, and unlike his brother and sister, he didn't get trashed, so I killed him and his young family. He is my biggest regret. I hated what it did to Phoebe. I may have wanted her bank balance and lifestyle but I also liked her. She had good business sense and, unlike me, she had compassion.

As for Damian, he was everything Phoebe and Alex weren't. He treated Calliope abysmally. I might be a murderer, but I make it quick and where possible, painless. I doubt Damian knew anything after he slipped and bashed his head. He was already unconscious when I found him, I just finished the job.

Calliope, on the other hand, felt every punch he delivered, and her heart broke a little more with every cruel word he ever said to her, and there were plenty of each. That made the blood go to my head. He deserved a far more horrific death then he got.

Daphne, well, she was a walnut from a different walnut. I actually liked her; she was a lot like Phoebe, but she was too sad. It was better that she go quietly than destroy everything Phoebe had built. I knew it would be the end of Phoebe, who had been sinking deeper and deeper into depression since Alex and his family died. And with only Daphne left, Phoebe had clung to her, but she was clinging to something fragile that could, and would break under the weight of such need.

Would I do anything differently? Yes, all of it. I live in a house full of ghosts. My wife, whom I love dearly, is still only a shadow of her former self, and my own children, well let's just say Daphne and Damian's legacy continues under my roof. I know how Phoebe felt, as history repeats itself, and I wonder if the land is cursed."

Andros bowed his head, and a single tear found its way into his cognac. Azrael looked at each of his guests allowing an unworldly silence to drift uncomfortably over them.

# CHAPTER XXV
## JAI

The silence continued to linger. It carried with it the threat of a decision, the threat of imminent death.

It could have been seconds, minutes or longer. Conventional time had little meaning in this place. The only time that really mattered was the years taken from tonight's sacrificial lamb.

Jai knew he had to tell his version of the events that had brought him here, to Lucretia's on the Hill.

Azrael's eyes flashed around the room before settling on Jai. The two stared at each other, almost lost in the silence. It was Azrael who eventually spoke.

"You know, Jai, you may well be damned if you do, but you will almost certainly be damned if you don't."

Perhaps he had taken his time answering, knowing that following his defence a decision would be made, and that this may well be the last time he would ever speak.

He took a deep breath, centred himself and began his defence.

"I honestly hadn't meant for it to go so far. When I suggested Ekansh and I switch places, it was only meant to be one last prank. I truly believed that they would realise I wasn't the right boy and send me back.

I was fully prepared for a life on the streets. What I was not prepared for was the merchant, Arman Sayani. You see, I like men. I had always loved Ekansh, but secretly. I never told him, and besides I know he longed for a wife. Ekansh was infatuated by one of the girls at the orphanage.

Mr Sayani, Arman, was a different matter. He was still quite young and he was beautiful, and I could see that he liked me. He said he wanted to interview me alone, and throughout the interview he touched my leg several times. Each time his hand moved further up towards my genitals. I was as stiff as a dead rat, and he could see me through my dhoti and eventually he could no longer resist. We made love all that afternoon and I knew then that I could never go back. Not only because I had fallen for Arman but also because I knew

Ekansh would be out of his depth. It was a total mess, and I was, as you said earlier, damned whatever I did.

I did not know what happened to Ekansh once he left the orphanage. I had hoped he had found work elsewhere, but in my heart I knew it was unlikely. I also knew that sooner or later Karma would catch up with me, and I guess now it has.

If I am to be the sacrifice, then so be it. Kali is both creator and destroyer and I will offer her my life, should she wish it."

# JUDGEMENT

# CHAPTER XXVI
## TWELVE GOOD MEN AND TRUE

"Tonight, all that remains is for you to decide which of you is to be the sacrifice. In a twist of irony, you now become the twelve good men and true. It is for you all to decide who among you is to be sacrificed.

You have until the morning to deliberate on your collective fate. It is midnight now, so shall we say 6 am? That gives you 6 hours to deliberate.

Samael, Iblis' hourglass please."

Samael returned carrying a large hourglass, filled with blood-red sand, which he placed in the centre of the table where it was visible to all. Azrael clapped his hands and the daughters returned with a ballot box, papers and pens.

"When the last grain of sand slips through the neck you must cast your vote and we will count them. The one who has the most votes will be the sacrifice. We shall leave you to it."

Azrael, Samael and the daughters of Iblis left via the only visible doorway—the one to the kitchen.

And so, they sat all night discussing who among them had committed the worst crimes. Which one of them deserved to die, over and above all the others.

There was little doubt that some crimes seemed worse than others, but that very much depended upon who you asked. Each one of them defended their lives to the last and condemned each other's just as fiercely.

Simon was the first to speak, coming across as more angry than afraid.

"So, we are the accused and jury—I swear these people are just as bad as we are, if not worse."

"I think that's the point, Simon, don't you?" Isobella offered. "None of us are sin free and all of us only ever think of ourselves. It's quite clever when you think about it."

"Clever? It's insane."

"No, Simon, it's clever. Think about it. We have been chosen because we are direct descendants of those who originally founded the twelve tribes of Israel. Do any of you know how long ago that was?"

"Around 4,000 years ago, give or take. That's what Azrael said." Danyl was the only one to offer a tangible date. Lewis suggested last week, and while it wasn't anywhere near accurate, it was no further from the actual date than Ruby's offering of shortly after the dinosaurs.

"Biblically I believe it was 3,224 to be as near to accurate as it gets, but around 4,000 is definitely close enough."

"Is there a point to this?"

"Yes, of course." Isobella frowned at Jai. She would hardly have said it if there wasn't a point to it.

"My point is, just how many descendants do you suppose there are kicking around? Zillions, right? And of those, how many do you suppose will have committed worse crimes than us? Thousands, possibly even millions, wouldn't you say? So, why us? My guess is because we are selfish and cruel.

Psychopaths are born deranged, we weren't. Neither are we sociopaths.

We are, in fact, the products of anger, jealousy, lust, pride, laziness, greed and gluttony. To some extent or other we represent every sin in the book. Perhaps that's what they are looking for—biblical sins, and more importantly, biblical sinners.

And then factor in our crimes with the ten commandments: I, the Lord, am your God. You shall not have any other gods besides me. Well, that's easy, I'm guessing this one is levied at you Jai—Hindu, yes?"

Jai shrugged. He could hardly be held responsible for the beliefs of his country.

Isobella continued undeterred. "You shall not take the name of the Lord, your God, in vain. So, how many of you are blasphemers? How many times have your actions shown a lack of love and respect for your god, or in your case, Jai, gods? For example, Zack, when you left those people to starve to death, did that show devotion to your god? Do you believe you acted righteously? And that applies to all of us—"

"I have always done what the Lord asked of me," Simon quickly interjected, not wishing to be tarred with that particular brush.

"Really, Simon? Letting young women die in pain is showing respect for your god is it? According to your beliefs, he created them too, you know.

Where was I? Oh yes, remember to keep holy the Sabbath day. I actually think that I'm the only one who may have even come close to keeping this commandment, and I did a piss poor job of it.

Honour your father and mother. I'm pretty sure that none of us kept this commandment. Even those of us whose parents were good people and deserved honour, have been dishonoured by our actions."

"Actually, Miss know-it-all, my parents have always been proud of me and I of them."

"OK, Simon, if you say so." Isobella continued undeterred. "What about thou shall not kill? Did you keep that one too? Did you show respect for the life of others by caring for all of God's creatures, especially people? And, Simon, think long and hard before you leap in with how you took an oath to save life.

And what about thou shall not commit adultery? This is about showing respect for your body and the bodies of others. Can you honestly say you use your body in a way that would please God?

And thou shall not steal. For fucks sake, Jai stole someone's entire identity. We have stolen money, lives, childhoods and sex.

Thou shall not bear false witness. I think we can say we are well and truly guilty of this one."

Simon and Danyl both opened their mouths, but Isobella scowled at them, and both thought better of it.

"Thou shall not covet your neighbour's wife, or husband, Ruby."

Ruby wanted to argue but knew there was nothing she could say.

"And finally, thou shall not covet anything that belongs to your neighbour—Andros. I think we can see why we are here, can't we?"

"Look," whispered Ruby. "The sand. It's nearly time to vote." They looked at each other, unable to decide who might vote for who. It was every man and woman for themselves.

# CRIME AND PUNISHMENT

# CHAPTER XXVII
## A LAST WORD

As the last grain of sand filtered through the neck of the hourglass, Azrael resumed his place as Master of Ceremonies.

This time, however, Azrael and his assistants had lost their glamours, and with them, their beautiful human appearance. The angel of death is not a beautiful man, nor does he come with white feathery wings. He has been doing this job since the dawn of time. He is not beautiful because death is not beautiful. The slaughtering of the first born, wiping out Sodom and Gomorrah, and the destruction of the Nephilim had all taken their tolls, and the darkness of his own atrocities was what the guests now saw.

Samael, too, had returned to his natural grotesque state, and where once three beautiful women had waited on them, three fire spirits now replaced them. The elder daughters of Iblis guarding the door, likewise, had returned to their shadow selves with flames instead of eyes.

Azrael's voice was now as formidable as his appearance. His angry tone, which at times had seemed almost musical, had been replaced by something far more terrifying, something more dreadful—a sinister, menacing rasp. It was as though all the souls whose lives he had ended were screaming to be released.

"Thirteen cups of Old Reviver please, daughters of Iblis, before we take a look at the votes."

This time, when the daughters returned with the coffee, they were followed by a young woman.

"Please allow me to introduce the owner, and your chef for this evening, Lucretia, the abused woman." Azrael announced. "I'm sure Isobella, at least, is familiar with her sorrowful story. It comes from Ancient Rome, and is one of rape, suicide and vengeance."

Once the coffee was placed on the table, Azrael, Samael, the daughters of Iblis, and Lucretia, the abused woman, counted the votes. There was much whispering and muttering from the hosts, but only minutes later they fell silent. Azrael took a sip of coffee and looked deep into the eyes of each of the guests. He could see the darkness in what remained of their souls, and he could smell their fear; he knew exactly what was in their hearts.

When Azrael addressed the room this time, it was as if the legions of Hell spoke through him, and his guests remained silent. They had been paralysed with fear since he and the others had returned. It was obvious their use of human glamour had been intended to lull them into a false sense of security. There was no such requirement now.

"I believe, my little sinners, that it is decision time. The evening is over and with it the wait. I believe you have all made the right decision, but I'm sure you are all aware that we would override it should we choose to do so.

However, tonight I sense we are in agreement, but that means nothing to any of you yet, does it? Sam, daughters, and Lucretia if you wouldn't mind."

He scanned the room, watching the guests' faces as a demon, five djinn and the abused woman shackled each one into their seats with heavy chains and several locks. A few might have considered running for the kitchen door, but it was never going to be more than a flight of fancy—the doorway ceased to exist long before the thought had properly formulated within their minds.

"It would be valiant but futile—shooting fish in a barrel, and where's the sport in that?" Azrael smiled, amused by their thoughts.

"Now, let me begin with Jai. Little Jai, you who are guilty of so many lies, and so much deception and of course, the horrors it inflicted. Ekansh's blood is on your hands. You may not have loaded the needle or sawn off his leg, but you are most definitely the cause of his death. I could let you leave here today, but it will cost you. I would demand of you that you fund a shelter for homeless teenagers. You are to honour your friend's legacy instead of disgracing yourself further, because when Karma speaks, it speaks loudly and it means every word, and today, I am Karma." His voice grew much louder and more threatening towards the end of his sentence and his smile exposed sharp, jagged, oversized teeth.

"And Zack, poor misunderstood Zack just wanted Daddy's approval. But all those babies—you were supposed to care for the helpless not leave them to starve to death. And the screams of those poor people burned alive. How do you sleep at night? You are an exceptional kind of evil and it would take a miracle for you to walk out of here tonight. However, if by some obscure twist of fate you do escape with your life, I expect you to run New Babylon as it was intended— as a safe haven, not as a death camp.

And Isobella, beautiful, horrible Isobella. Those innocents came to you seeking holy guidance and instead found abuse. And all the while you knew their fate, you took the money, and drank and whored away your guilt." Azrael paused and looked quizzically at Isobella. "Did it help? Did the relentless booze, sex and abortions in some way alleviate your conscience?" Isobella opened her mouth to speak but the daughters collectively put a finger to their mouths and shushed her. "Your crimes leave such a foul taste, but were I to consider freeing you, you and I both know that I would expect you to be the right type of Catholic.

And so, we come to Lewis, twisted in so many ways. You were an angry little boy, and you are an angry man. You literally treated your wife, both your sons and those little children in Iraq like rats. And not even the decency to bury them. Your wife and children were wrapped in an old rug and left to rot in a cellar. These people loved you, and that is how you honour them. As for those children in Iraq, their chopped up little bodies were just left for hungry dogs and other scavengers. I can see no reason to show you any mercy, but should I find one, I expect you to confess your crimes, accept the consequences and lay your family properly to rest."

Lewis nodded sheepishly.

"Oh, that's not all! At the very least I would expect you to sell your house and donate the proceeds along with all your savings to build a domestic abuse shelter for the victims of violence. I find you quite revolting and I expect you to be making amends forever."

Andros, you have so much more financially than Lewis, but you also have much to atone for and you have proved how devious and calculating you can be. Poor little Daphne and sad old Phoebe, such heartache and for what? To line your pockets. Tell me, Andros, are your parents proud of you? What? Can't hear you—cat got your tongue? I have no desire whatsoever to release you, but in the unlikely event I find a reason to do so, you will pay—dearly. You will open a drug rehabilitation centre in Daphne's name, not yours, and you will take no credit for it. Likewise, you will donate 50% of your earnings to charity. Half of this will form a fund in Phoebe's name to counsel bereaved parents, the other half will go to victims of fraud."

He was playing with them; they could see that now. The invitation, the exclusive restaurant, the menu, the servile pretences of Samael and the daughters of Iblis had all been nothing more than a deadly game of cat and mouse, and the cats were more lethal and more deadly than ever.

The demon, the djinn and the abused woman revelled in the atmosphere of panic and despair, so thick they could taste it. Catching sight of Samael licking his lips, Azrael continued his monologue.

"Nathan, sweet, affable Nathan. The only one of you who extended his hand to greet me first. A gentle giant, or so you would have us believe. But my, there's a darkness beneath that friendly exterior that grows more dangerous by the day. You are an arsonist, a murderer, a glory hunter and a coward. How many died in those fires you set? I doubt you can even remember. You were lucky that last little girl survived—any longer and she wouldn't have. It has become all too easy for you, setting fires, letting your colleague die; you have become desensitised and human life means precious little.

If I were to allow you to leave this place, I would require that you seek employment elsewhere, and that you pay your colleague's family the compensation they deserve. Let's say, 25% of your income—don't look at me like that or I'll double it—25% is reasonable, after all your wife and stepdaughter don't need to suffer, they are innocent, and I am not a monster.

And next is the lost little German boy, poor Julian carrying so much guilt it weighs you down, and so it should. The suffering you have caused, the deaths you have caused, not to mention all those junkie whores that you introduced to the world of heroin addiction. You took their lives, their virginity, and worse still, you took their souls. Some were barely old enough but why let that stop you? Why should I even consider sparing your wretched life?"

Julian opened his mouth to answer but was instantly shushed with a look from the daughters of Iblis,

"Should I find a way to justify releasing you, then you will make some amends by opening a safehouse for the victims of people like you. You will help the junkie whores of Berlin's underworld, rescuing as many as possible. You know enough to convict those further up the criminal food chain, therefore become an informant. If you are lucky, you may get witness protection. If you are not, well perhaps that could be considered justice.

Ruby, the adulteress and fornicator, incapable of love and compassion. You have used and spat out so many lovers, viewing their wedding rings as a safety net—after all you don't need them to leave their wives or husbands, just amuse you for a while. It doesn't matter who gets hurt along the way, as long as it isn't you, right?

Should I consider letting you go, it will only be on the proviso that, like the others, you make changes. You will use some of your wealth to fund the welfare clinic where Dr Angela worked and ensure that there is enough staff to make a proper difference on Skid Row. It should go without saying that you will refrain from sex with those who are married."

Ruby nodded. She knew this may well be her last few hours of life. She had no words, just an empty hope.

Azrael shifted his gaze to focus on Gerry, who was beyond uncomfortable.

"You are nothing more than a rapist and wife beater. What you did to your wives and baby daughter is unforgiveable. The abuse you put Jane and Alex through and the brutal death of Mary—you have no justification for your actions, and I have no incentive to let you leave here. However, as with all of you, should fate decree you are to be freed, there will be conditions. In your case, I would demand that you turn yourself in, admit your guilt and allow your wives and baby to be properly laid to rest. Furthermore, while in prison, you are to seek anger management therapy, and in the unlikely event of you ever being released, you would be required to voluntarily help victims of abuse."

Gerry looked at Azrael and could see the contempt in his eyes; there was no choice but to accept his fate.

Azrael was swift to move on. "Ah, Ben. What to do with Ben? On the one hand, such a wasted gift and on the other hand, I would sacrifice you in a heartbeat—if I had a heart, that is. Fortunately, I do not. But those you have murdered or infected did, and they trusted you. Some even loved you. In order for you to ever leave here you would be spending the rest of your life celibate. Of course, I could release you on the proviso that you used contraception but that would be too easy, as would either chemical or physical castration. I want you to suffer as you have caused others to suffer. So, I will secure you a place in a Buddhist monastery where you will learn how to control your sexual desires. It will be much harder, excuse the pun, than you imagine."

Azrael was enjoying this, that much was obvious. He was relishing their fear and they in turn hated him. Each of them dangling on a thread, knowing that for one of them there was no escape.

"Eeny, meeny, miney, Simon. Such a pillar of the community; a wonderful husband and father who, unlike most here tonight, had a charmed upbringing. However, despite your privileged childhood, you are a murderer of young women. It is also true that some of these are not yet women. You refuse to help them, instead taking their lives, one way or another. And why? Because your god requires it. No god requires 12-year-old rape victims to be forced to give birth, not even a jumped-up little desert god like Yahweh. I have no cause to let you go, but if by some miracle you escape being sacrificed, I would see you working in a welfare clinic helping girls in need. Yes, Simon, that means performing abortions. And before you say anything—don't!"

Azrael glared at Simon, almost daring him to speak, but for the first time that evening he bit his tongue and remained silent.

"Danyl, my little junkie fiend. I see you beginning to shake and sweat and of course we *could fix* that for you, but we won't—I would be lying if I said we didn't enjoy your suffering."

Danyl could see them all watching him, and the daughters licked their lips almost lasciviously, in that collective way of theirs.

"You have caused so much suffering, Danyl, and for a good Jewish boy you have broken so many commandments. What must the rabbis think? You have dishonoured the memory of not only your mother and father, but also your grandmother and grandfather. You have stolen, killed and blasphemed. Or do you believe your actions in some way honour your god? And then, there is the blackmail. Your crimes are many and like everyone else here, you don't really deserve another chance. But should mercy prevail, you will get clean, admit your crimes and pay for

the murder of your wife and child. You
will never be released from prison but
you can help other addicts in there.”

For all of them chained up
around the table, death was growing
ever closer.

# CHAPTER XXVIII
## THE SACRIFICE

"It seems we have reached the end of the evening, and one of you is to remain here. Of course, myself and my companions would willingly sacrifice all of you." The fire in the younger daughters' eyes glowed with delight at the prospect, as did Samael's. The elder daughters of Iblis remained just as stoic and formidable as they had all evening.

"What a delicious idea, Azreal. You're such a tease," Lucretia whispered seductively, wringing her hands in anticipation.

"The beauty of this evening is that although you all voted, you will never know whether it was your vote that condemned tonight's blasphemy offering or whether it was our decision that was the final nail in their coffin."

The look of delight on their faces was matched by the look of horror on the faces of their guests.

"You see, ultimately what condemns a person is the consequences of their actions. On the surface, Zack's crimes may seem worse than those of Ruby or Simon, but perhaps the little girl who died in the alleyway that night as a result of Ruby's behaviour might have grown up to find a cure for cancer. Or that young girl Simon left to die in agony might have become the mother of someone responsible for world peace.

Simon wanted to speak but Azrael put his finger to his lips.

"Hush!" he rasped. "I know you wish to protest but the awful truth is, your protesting is why you are here tonight. Everyone else knows they are guilty, but you don't see that you have done anything wrong. God loves you, huh? Where is your god now?

Just to be absolutely clear, leaving here is not supposed to be an easy option. You are as guilty as it gets, you wouldn't be here if you weren't. Failure to comply with any of my demands will, of course, see you suffer tenfold. And this applies to all of you," he growled. "Should any of you leave here and fail to make proper recompense, you will, without exception, become the victims of your own crimes. And make no mistake, we will be watching you—at all times."

I think it is time now, don't you?" Azrael was no longer addressing the guests but his companions as he had called them. The demon, the shayāṭīn and Lucretia clapped their hands and the chains of those to be released fell to the floor. The doors to the outside world reappeared and the guests made a hasty exit.

Ruby was the last to leave. She took a final look at Simon, the man she had voted for, as the daughters of Iblis strapped him to the dinner table. Azrael gestured for her to close the door behind her, and as she did so, she could have sworn she heard Lucretia's voice. Despite the door being closed, Ruby heard the words clearly enough.

"OK boys and girls, let's play doctors and nurses!"